No Pucks Lost Between Us

Rush Hockey #6

Elise Faber

NO PUCKS LOST BETWEEN US
BY ELISE FABER

Newsletter sign-up

Rush Hockey

Big Puck Energy
Filthy Puckboy
So Pucking Over It
Love, Pucks, and Other Stories
All's Fair in Pucks and War
No Pucks Lost Between Us
Puck and Make Up

PROLOGUE

BILLIE ROSE

The metal had bitten into my wrists, leaving harsh bruises. The air was chilled, prickling goose bumps on my arms.

The smell was awful—a combination of BO and urine and rotten food.

Even the lights glared down at me.

But the noise...

That was the worst.

Banging and shouting. Singing and screaming. Constant chattering and phones ringing and...cell doors slamming shut.

A cacophony of stimulation that grated every second.

And that never stopped.

Just...a constant barrage to my senses.

And all the while, my fear morphed into other emotions.

Confusion and rage and—

Acceptance.

Because what had happened was inevitable—me being tied to

the train tracks, stuck, frozen in place as the heavy steel engine barreled down on me.

Closer. Closer.

Boom.

ONE

BILLIE ROSE

"Yo, bitch!"

I inhaled, shuddered, didn't lift my head from my knees.

I'd already made that mistake in the hours I'd been locked in this cell.

I wasn't making it again.

"*Yo, bitch!*"

The clang was louder this time, making me jump, almost impossible to ignore, but I just shoved my forehead harder against my kneecaps, as though I could roll myself up into a ball, pretend that this hadn't actually happened.

But it had.

My dad had set me up to take the fall...for something.

Something big and bad and with dire consequences—

Hence the reason my ass was sitting in this jail cell, trying to be as small as possible, trying to not garner any attention, trying not to—

"*Yo, bitch!*"

Jesus Christ.

My head shot up, eyes searching for the source of the screaming, connecting with the woman in the next cell over.

"What'd ya do?" she hollered.

"I have no fucking clue," I muttered, dropping my head back onto my knees.

There was no way she should have been able to hear me, not over the cacophony of sounds.

But she must have, or anticipated what I was going to say. Or —hell—maybe she could read lips. Whatever the reason, she called, "It'll be okay, baby girl. We've all been there!"

Framed for a crime I hadn't committed.

By my father.

So...no. I doubted that she'd been there.

Creak!

I jerked my head up again, but this time I didn't search for the source of the sound. I knew it was the heavy metal cell door swinging open, and my stomach immediately clenched. Because I'd been by myself until now, locked up separately from the other inmates in the county jail.

Only now, there was a woman who looked like she could crush me between thumb and forefinger, strolling into the cell like she owned the place.

And—who was I kidding?—her sheer size alone meant that she did.

"Donovan!"

My head whipped to the side, away from the behemoth with the scowling expression—and I saw an officer standing in the opening.

He signaled to me. "Follow me."

I didn't know if I was about to be interrogated.

I *did* know I wanted the fuck away from the behemoth. Especially because she was cracking her knuckles, rolling her shoulders, her big bones rolling and jumping.

Right.

I hopped to my feet, hurried toward the officer and the open cell door.

Behemoth chuckled, rotating her neck, sending the vertebrae inside crunching.

I picked up my pace, nearly running into the officer, who didn't look the least bit bothered by the scary, scary woman.

"Come on," he said, after sliding the cell door closed with a *clang*.

I trailed him down the hall, realizing this was probably my time for my one phone call.

Bailey.

I'd call my niece.

Not the man I loved, not Joel. He was supposed to be focused on his own life, his own career. It was the playoffs for River's Bend hockey team, the Rush, and they had an important game tonight. I didn't need to distract him from that.

He could yell at me later.

After they'd won.

Bailey, definitely. But I'd swear her to secrecy...

Which wouldn't do shit.

Because she'd tell her professional hockey playing husband who'd tell my professional hockey playing boyfriend and—

Games and lives would be disrupted.

Dessie then. My other best friend outside of Bailey.

She'd keep her mouth shut and—

"Bailey."

I nearly jumped out of my skin.

We'd entered a small room, where I'd been anticipating finding nothing but two-way glass, a phone, and another police officer who'd be blatantly listening in on my conversation.

I hadn't expected the man I barely knew.

I hadn't expected Joel's father, Rob.

Except...he was a lawyer.

Let me just curl up into a ball and die a thousand deaths as embarrassment impaled me again and again and *again*.

"How are you here?" I whispered.

"Dessie called Bailey who called Joel"—my eyes slid closed—"who called me. I hopped on a flight, which was why it took me so long to get up here," he said softly. "Sorry, I couldn't make it sooner."

"Joel knows?"

Rob nodded. "He's outside."

My hands started shaking, eyes stinging. I'd been scared out of my mind, avoiding thinking about what was happening, sitting in my rage, in my fury because of my father's betrayal, in my confusion and horror and the sadness that this was happening at all. "But he's supposed to be playing tonight."

Rob had been rolling back the top sheet of a legal pad, uncapping a pen.

My statement had him freezing. "You needed him, Rosie."

As though that were expectation enough.

And...I supposed it was.

Joel was a protector, the man who loved me. He wouldn't leave me alone in a jail cell, not if he could do anything to get me out of it. But, "The playoffs," I whispered.

Rob put down the pen, took my hand. "Hockey will never be more important than you."

My lungs went tight because...

That wasn't my life. I wasn't important—or at least, not more important than the responsibilities of a team needing him. Not more important than Joel's job and livelihood. Not more important than my town, than my people—

"Rosie."

I looked up.

Rob studied my expression then shook his head, fingers squeezing mine. "Later," he murmured, almost to himself. "Okay, honey, so bond has been posted, which means you'll be out of here shortly."

"I—" But I cut myself off, knowing already who would have done that for me.

Joel.

The man who loved me.

The same man who sent his father.

After *my* father had fucked me over.

The irony...was painful.

Rob squeezed my fingers again. "I'll get a copy of the arrest report, find out what charges are going to be filed, and then we'll sort this all out."

"I don't think I've done anything," I whispered. "I followed every rule, tried to help my town—"

"Later," he said again.

And I realized a heartbeat after the word hit the air it was because the door was opening.

"Billie Rose?" I swiveled in my chair, saw Dave, still in uniform, the police chief much less crisply pressed than he'd been hours earlier when he'd arrested me. "You're free to go. Mr. Marshall"—a nod to Joel's father—"has the information for your court date. If you follow me, we'll grab your things and get you out of here."

I nodded, stood, started to move to the door.

Rob snagged my arm, halting me. "What's the situation like out front?" he asked Dave.

Dave sighed. "Still a shit show."

I glanced between them, frowned. "What's a shit show?"

"The press are outside," Rob explained then glanced back at Dave. "You'll let us leave out the back door?"

Dave flicked his eyes toward me and nodded then started down the hall again.

"You go with him, get your things," he murmured. "I'll come back with Joel, and we'll get you the hell out of here."

"Okay," I whispered.

A squeeze of my shoulder.

"This will all work out." He dropped his hand. "You'll see."

I highly doubted that.

But I just nodded and followed Dave down the hall.

Two

JOEL

I was ready to burst the door my dad had disappeared through. I'd only seen him for a minute, after renting a car and then driving like hell to get back here.

I loved my job, loved playing hockey, but getting that call from Bailey, hearing what had happened and not being here, not being close, not being in a position to get to Rosie quickly had made me hate it with a fucking passion.

Her life was imploding and I was twiddling my thumbs, navigating roads and traffic because it was faster to drive straight home than to an airport and rent a car and then drive another hour to River's Bend.

But those five hours had killed.

Even knowing my dad had dropped everything to get there first—though not by much, since he'd had to do the fly, drive an hour option.

Bailey, my woman's niece, wasn't in town.

She was traveling with her NHLer of a husband, who were in their own playoff matchup.

And Dessie, their other best friend, was on her first vacation in years, having only heard about the arrest through the gossip that flew through the small town of River's Bend swifter than the snowmelt rushing in early April.

My Rosie.

Alone.

Fucking again.

It made me want to put a fist through the wall.

Especially considering the assholes with their cameras outside were just dying to get a fucking shot of her.

"Joel."

I glanced away from the wide plate glass windows of the police station, dragging my gaze through the no longer pristine lobby, the space almost entirely brand-new after the huge fire had destroyed the town almost two years before. My Rosie had fought to get this space built, get the community put back together, to make sure River's Bend was as close as possible to what it had been before.

And she'd made it better.

Until someone had begun to systematically dismantle that.

I had my suspicions who.

I just...didn't know if those suspicions would help.

My dad waved me over and I followed him through that door and into the back, through the sea of desks, beyond these people that my woman who had fought so hard for and who had turned on her so fucking easily.

"Brace yourself, son," my dad muttered.

My fury went icy cold, dread joining the party. "For what?" I rasped.

"Just brace, stay calm, and we'll deal with it all when we've gotten her out of here and someplace safe."

Fury faded. Dread grew, morphed into something akin to panic that clawed at the back of my throat, but I battled it down, nodded firmly. "I'm fine."

My dad paused, studied me, then squeezed my shoulder.

"Good."

We turned the corner and I saw my woman's curly blonde hair. It was a mess in a way that I knew she'd never normally allow outside of the bedroom, outside of the soft slice of vulnerable she only gave me. To the outside world she was self-assured, confident, calm, and completely capable in a crisis.

The perfect mayor.

Who'd been arrested.

Her clothes—typical slacks and a button-down—were wrinkled and dirty, and she was wearing a pair of black flat leather shoes I knew she hated, but that she wore anyway because they were professional-looking and comfortable. Her head was down, curls bouncing slightly as she signed a paper an officer was pointing at, nodding in response before passing the pen back, gathering the papers, and looking up—

Rage shot through me, head to toes to fingertips. Red hazed into my vision.

"What the fuck?" I hissed.

"Later, son," my dad ordered softly, gripping my shoulder tightly enough that a bolt of pain shot through me.

Not trying to hurt me.

But...it banked my anger, that jab of hurt, helped me reign myself back in.

I glanced at my dad who nodded, murmured, "Later."

A breath, throwing the lock on my emotions, on the absolute rage that was roiling beneath the surface, and moved to my woman.

Who had a fucking black eye and scrape down one cheek.

That lock threatened to give way when I got closer and she turned to face me, when I could see the bleakness in her pretty blue eyes, when I got a better glimpse of that bruise and the cut on her cheek.

I was going to murder someone.

Give these fucking cops a real reason to lock one of us up.

But I was going to do it after I made sure she was safe and secure and—

Tears welled up in her eyes and I realized I'd paused a few feet away from her, probably giving her some sort of terrible silent message.

Quickly, I closed the distance between us, drew her into my arms. "You're okay, Rosie baby," I murmured into her ear when she came stiffly. "We're okay," I added when she didn't relax. "It's all going to be okay, I promise."

"You don't know that," she whispered back.

I *didn't* know that.

I just had to trust that it was the truth because she needed to hear it and I needed to say it.

"It's going to be okay," I said again, this time more firmly.

"Right," she replied softly, and I knew she didn't really believe it, because she didn't relax against me, she didn't settle into my embrace like she normally did. She just stood there for a moment, my arms around her, before she stepped back and asked quietly, "Can we go home?"

"Yeah, Rosie baby." I glanced toward my dad, who nodded. "I'll move my car around. Wait until I text you, yeah?"

"Right," I muttered.

He disappeared, and we stood there in our awkward, tense embrace until my phone buzzed with a text from him. "Let's go home."

An officer led us to the back door, pushed it open.

I moved us quickly to the rear of my dad's car, to the passenger's side door that was already open, tucked us inside. There was a commotion and a flurry of flashes, but by then I'd snagged the handle, tugged the metal panel closed.

My dad took off through the parking lot. "Buckle up."

I clicked us in just as we turned right onto Main Street.

Leaving a crowd of reporters behind us.

And the truth still very much hidden in the shadows.

THREE

BILLIE ROSE

I don't know what I expected.

I'd been arrested, thrown in a cell for hours.

But Joel's entryway littered with belongings, the floor marred with dirty footprints, wasn't something I anticipated. I wanted a bath and to go to bed, to sleep for a hundred hours. Not...this.

Not... I shifted out of the circle of his arms, moved to the side.

And my stomach clenched.

Because the ground floor of Joel's house was open concept.

Which meant that from three feet inside his front door, I could see everything—the kitchen, the great room, the dining nook, the large windows that were dark sheets of glass at the moment, but when the sun was up, revealed a huge wraparound deck that sat above a background that Joel had worked his ass off to make beautiful.

After the fire had torn everything away from him.

And now...

It was a fucking disaster.

The footprints were everywhere. But that wasn't what was bad, what was horrible. It was everything else.

Every drawer and cabinet in the kitchen was open, their contents scattered.

The vase I'd put daisies in just a few days before sat on its side, the flowers removed, strewn on the counter, the floor, their petals crushed into the wooden planks.

The basket my parents had dropped off a few days ago—a peace offering from my mom, who knew what from my dad—had been pulled open, the containers clearly rifled through. Stools were overturned, the fridge door had been left open and was beeping intermittently.

The cushions ripped off the couch, tossed on the floor, books astray, furniture out of place.

Even our jackets had been removed from the hooks in the entry, dumped onto the floor, the little basket I kept on a small table askew.

"It's just a mess," Joel murmured. "We'll get it cleaned up in the morning."

My gaze slid down the hall and I saw the sliver of light glinting off the floor.

I sucked in a breath.

"What?" he murmured, reaching for me.

But I was already moving, sprinting down the hall, pushing into my office...and skidding to a stop, heart breaking.

This space had been *my* space.

My safe space.

The one room that was mine, created for me by the man who loved me. A demonstration of that love, of his care and thoughtfulness, of...him and I together. The person I could be when I was with him. The woman who deserved that much love and care and—

Him.

And that was...

Gone.

Scattered like the rolls of washi tape on the floor.

Torn like the special stickers Joel had commissioned for me.

Stained like the cushy, and way too expensive rug he'd bought to make this room cozy.

Tipped over like the chairs I'd curled up in so freaking often, reading late into the night.

Destroyed.

I exhaled, blinked back tears, but then Joel was there, his strong arm banding around my middle, drawing me back against his chest.

"Shh," he whispered, turning me, weaving his hands into my hair, tucking my head beneath his chin. "It's fine. It's going to be fine."

"It's not f-fine." Shit. My voice cracked, tears clinging to my lashes, killing me. I needed to be strong and calm and focused. I needed to be all of those things so Joel would be comfortable leaving me to handle the pile of shit heaped on my lap. I needed to be all of those, so he wouldn't worry, so he could play hockey, so he could live out his dream without my stuff fucking up his life.

He'd already had more than enough to deal with over the last year.

What with his ex-wife showing up.

What with finding out he wasn't actually divorced...and supposed to be.

What with a fucking fire burning down his house.

I clenched my hands into fists, digging my nails into my palms, and struggled for control. It worked. The pain centered me, allowed me to focus, to *breathe.*

To stop the fucking tears before they escaped any further.

To wall up my emotions.

To just breathe and think and then...to pull out of the circle of his arms.

I turned for the hall, found myself stayed by a hand on my

shoulder. "Rosie baby," he said gently, so fucking gently that I nearly lost all that hard-fought control I'd just managed to obtain.

"I'm just going to grab some trash bags and the broom," I whispered, tugging at his hold.

"We should get some rest."

"*You* should get some rest," I countered. "You were the one on a bus half the night last night and up early on the ice this morning."

"I didn't make it to the ice."

I cringed. "I know."

"Shit, Rosie baby," he murmured. "I didn't mean it like that."

"I know," I whispered.

Fingers on my chin, turning my face up to his. "I didn't mean it like that, baby."

"I know," I whispered again.

He flattened his palm on my jaw, leaned down and brushed his lips over mine. "Come on, sweetheart," he said softly, drawing back and taking my hand. "We're going to bed. Tomorrow we can worry about clean up," he added when I opened my mouth to protest, already drawing me down the hall.

"But—"

Suddenly, he'd spun back around, big body crowding mine, bumping me lightly back into the wall, palms pressed to either side of my head, bracketing me in, blocking me from the mess, from the rest of the world. "We're going to bed," he gritted out. "We're getting some fucking sleep. Because my dad will be back in the morning and so will Bailey and Axel and Dessie—"

"But—"

"Our house is about to be full, Rosie baby. The people who love you—and there are fucking many—are going to close ranks." He settled his forehead against mine. "So brace, sweetheart. Brace and get those fucking thoughts out of your head. Everyone who loves you *knows* you. Here"—he dropped a hand to the spot over my heart"—they know you *here,* and they know you love this town and them equally as much. They know you would never do anything to jeopardize that. So sit in that, breathe that in, fucking accept it. And then"—he bent that big, strong body of his, scooped me up, held me tight against his chest—"deal with the fact that I'm here and I'm not going to leave you to handle this on your own. Deal with the fact that I love you, and that means I'm right *fucking* here, that you're not going to pull some Mayoral Magic bullshit and wave your wand and make this all go away." He dropped me on the bed, bent over me, hands on either side of my head again, only horizontally this time. "*I'm* not going away. No matter how hard you push."

I inhaled.

Blinked rapidly.

"Okay?" he pressed.

"Okay," I whispered.

Because I knew I had no other choice except to tell him that.

Because I didn't know if I had any Mayoral Magic left and my wand had been broken, and I wasn't sure I *wouldn't* end up alone.

I just...didn't have the strength to go down that road.

To think about how broken I would be if I did.

So, I just let Joel kiss me, let him help me exchange my clothes for pajamas and tuck me beneath the messy blankets, let him turn off the lights, hiding the chaos of the bedroom.

And I let him hold me as we both fell asleep.

Even though it took a long, long time.

FOUR

JOEL

I swept the final bit of dirt into the dustpan and dumped it into the trash can.

It was the middle of the night.

Rosie was finally asleep.

But I didn't want her to wake up to a disaster of a house, and I'd wanted to watch tape from the game tonight—or last night, anyway.

The guys looked strong.

They'd won without issue, so strongly that I hadn't even been missed. Which, frankly, was a bit of a blow to the ego, but also the way it needed to be.

I set the broom aside, paused the tape our video coach had sent me, and surveyed the space.

I'd managed to put it back together—righting furniture, straightening shit in cabinets, closing up drawers and doors, and throwing out shit that had been torn or ruined or food that had been opened and dug through.

Including those tins of cookies that Rosie's mom had brought by not long before.

A welcome gift.

A housewarming present.

An overture of...

Something.

But, as always, when it came to Annie Donovan, it was clouded with confusion and discomfort and...bullshit.

Because she lived in a world shrouded with fog.

Because she'd never been there for her daughter.

Except, she'd approached me in the parking lot before I'd gotten on the bus for the game.

And she'd warned me about...John Donovan.

Billie's dad.

She'd warned me and—

I'd gotten on the fucking bus and my woman—

Had ended up in handcuffs, in a jail cell, with a black eye, with a cut on her cheek.

I bit back a curse, tugged out my earbuds, and shoved them into the case. I'd had enough tape, enough watching my teammates play in a game I should have been pulling my weight at.

I didn't regret coming back or resent my Rosie for having that need.

But I fucking hated the circumstances that had brought us to this moment—to the black eye and cut on her cheek, to the cleaning in the middle of the night, to the storm in my gut that told me I shouldn't have left her in the first place...

The storm that told me this was all just beginning.

And sighed.

Knowing that I needed to get my head on straight.

Knowing I needed to keep it that way.

I put on a pot of coffee, waited while it brewed, then carried my mug to the windows, staring out to the dark back yard. It wasn't pitch black any longer, the horizon having lightened just the slightest bit in the distance, a faint glow of orange coating a narrow strip of the foothills of the Sierra Nevadas.

Isolated, but not.

A quiet, peaceful slice of heaven...inhabited by a wolf.

Who sunk his teeth into my woman.

Christ.

I took a fortifying sip of coffee, and then another.

Calm. Breathe. Think. Protect—

The last word sliding through my mind had me freezing, plunking my mug on the side table and leaning forward, so close to the glass my nose almost bumped into it.

But...

The shadows were moving, forming...

At first I thought it might be a deer or a coyote or bobcat, but it was bigger than those. Maybe a bear or a mountain lion or—

No.

I was glad I'd put the mug down already because when my eyes adjusted and I realized—

I was sprinting toward the door on the deck.

Yanking it open with a crash that shook the house.

Pounding across the deck in bare feet, the cold of morning biting at the soles as I darted across the lawn, toward the tree line, but I hardly noticed the small jabs of pain.

Because I'd reached the trees.

And the person crawling toward me.

FIVE

BILLIE ROSE

The crash sent me bolt upright in bed, heart pounding as my gaze shot around the room.

I tried to find the source of the noise, the source of the terror that had sent me to sudden alertness, but it was dark and I was alone and—

I tossed the blankets back, stood, my temple and eye and cheek aching from my time in the jail cell—and my quickly learned from mistake of making eye contact with the wrong person. That had earned me a tray launched between the cell's bars and me...not dodging quickly enough.

Ibuprofen would be my friend.

As soon as I figured out what had awoken me and where the hell Joel was.

I flicked on the light, seeing—yup—that the room was empty.

I bent, just to double check, felt that the other side of the bed was cold, as was his pillow.

And then my heart began pounding for a completely different reason. Maybe he'd left. Maybe he'd left *me*—

"Stop," I whispered.

This was his house.

He wouldn't leave me.

If anything, he would be the one to order me out.

"Stop," I whispered again, more fully this time, turning away from the sight of that empty bed that had my bile rising in my throat, burning the back of it, sending my mind down a line of thinking I was almost desperate to cut off...

Turning away and nearly killing myself on a pile of our belongings on the floor.

Clothes and shoes tangled together.

My slacks and flats. Joel's jeans and boots.

Not a mess from the police searching our home.

Just the two of us being lazy and not putting our shit together.

And that sight—that normalcy—settled my pulse, eased some of the worry, allowed me to swallow, to soothe that burn in the back of my throat.

Stop. Think.

Don't react.

Don't run off.

Fight for what you want.

I wanted my life with Joel.

I wanted—

The bedroom door crashed open and I jumped, nearly tripping over the tangle of clothes and shoes again as I whipped toward it and saw Joel standing wild-eyed on the threshold.

"Rosie baby," he began and I took a step toward him, not nearly this time, but tripping, tumbling forward, watching the hardwood floor whip up toward my face, bracing.

Joel was there, catching me, drawing me against him.

Scooping me up like I weighed nothing.

And I knew—to him—I didn't.

Not my actual body mass, but also the weight of my responsibilities, the weight of what was barreling down on me with the arrest and charges and recall and petitions that had clogged up my desk, bogged down my job.

With my job that had me up at all hours and pulled away from him countless times.

And he'd never complained.

Because he respected what I did.

Because his job was important to him too.

Because—

I hadn't really processed we were moving, that he'd carried me from the room—mostly because I was having a realization that I was heading back down a path I'd struggled to traverse in the first place—thinking I had no value, that my only worth was what was good for the town, for the people. That I was my job and *only* my job.

How long had it taken for Joel to disabuse me of that notion?

Too fucking long.

And I'd fought too hard to get to a place where I viewed myself differently to go back now.

So...

Fuck that. I was *not* going back.

I'd had my little freak-out, my little bit of time to have my pity party.

That was done.

I was figuring out what in the fuck all was going on with my father and the job and me being fucking handcuffed and hauled away to jail and—

I started, thankful that Joel was holding me because the sight in the family room was one I would have never predicted, because if I'd been standing on my own two feet, I probably would have tripped again, would have needed to be saved from face planting into the hardwood a second time.

But that wasn't an issue.

Because I was still in Joel's arms, still cradled against his chest.

He slowly lowered me to my feet, hands remaining on my hips for a moment, steadying me.

But I only needed him for that moment.

After that, my brain caught up with the rest of my body, and I was rushing forward, moving toward the woman standing in our family room.

With bare feet.

In a threadbare nightgown that showed exactly how thin she'd become—something I'd failed to notice since I'd been so deliberately keeping her at a distance, shielding myself from the pain of her presence.

Her hair, that had once been blonde like mine, but was now more silver than anything, was tucked up in a bonnet she swore protected her curls.

It did.

I just could never be bothered to take the time to put one on.

The nightgown didn't cover her arms and it ended below her knees...and there were those bare feet again.

I finally snapped out of my stupor, moved to the mudroom, to our jackets—obliquely noticing they were back on the hooks, that the space was spotless, coupling that with Joel's side of the bed being cold and knowing my sweet, awesome man had been busy while I was sleeping.

Taking care of me.

Protecting me.

I glanced at Joel, who met my eyes with a blank stare until I flicked my gaze around the room then back to his.

He shrugged.

I narrowed my eyes.

We'd be having a talking to later.

Right now, I was avoiding.

Again.

Because I didn't want to deal with any of this—not the arrest or what my father was involved in, and what it meant for me.

And I didn't want to deal with the woman standing in my living room.

The history was too big, too heavy.

Too overwhelming and smothering and—

Avoiding.

Again.

I exhaled, gripped the jacket a little tighter...

And I walked over, slung it over...

My mother's shoulders.

Six

JOEL

Cuts and scratches riddled Annie's feet and legs and arms, but it was her eyes that were seriously unnerving.

Unfocused.

Distant.

Her face lax.

Like she'd been from the moment I reached her at the trees. She hadn't so much as flinched when I took her by the arm and drew her inside.

And she hadn't so much as moved from the spot since I'd paused in the kitchen, dropped my hold on her arm, and moved down the hall to get my Rosie.

Hadn't moved when I carried Rosie back, nor when she went and retrieved a jacket and wrapped it around her mother's shoulders.

She still wasn't moving now.

Her face remained lax, her gaze unfocused.

Rosie glanced back over her shoulder at me, brows lifted.

I shrugged, did the only thing I could think of—moved to the sink and pulled out the first aid kit from the cabinet beneath it.

Then I walked back over to the women.

Rosie had taken my cue—of course she had—wrapping her fingers around her mom's arm, drawing her over to a stool, nudging her down into it. I handed her a cleaning wipe, watched as she hesitated, then tore it open, dabbing at some of the worst wounds, watching as she opened her mouth, closed it, opened it again.

She exhaled, asked what I thought was the most pertinent question. "Why are you here?"

Annie flinched, the fog clearing.

She lifted her arm, almost in slow motion, and opened her hand, turning it palm up, and revealing...

A flash drive.

"What's that?" Rosie asked after a moment's pause.

"Evidence." Annie stood, jacket falling from her shoulders, turning and gripping Rosie's arms tightly enough to make my woman wince, shaking her so fiercely that I took a step toward them, intending to pull her free.

But then Rosie was slipping out of the hold, rotating and taking her mothers's hands, retrieving the flash drive. "Evidence of what, Mom?"

The fog started to slip back in.

I saw it creep onto the edges of Annie's expression, watched it settle into her eyes.

So did Rosie. "Mom. *Mom.*"

A blink. Clarity. "Evidence of your father's corruption," she whispered.

———

I pulled open the door just enough to allow my dad to make his way inside, but not far enough to give any of the photographers standing on the sidewalk, parked next to the curb, a glimpse into the house.

"Hey," I said softly as I shut and locked the door. "Thanks for coming, Pops."

My dad clapped me lightly on the shoulder. "No thanks needed, son. Not now. Not ever."

I exhaled.

My dad had joked not long ago that he was great at giving Dad—and it was true. He was steady, easy, and there had never been a moment in my life where I questioned his love for me, questioned that he liked me, questioned that he would be there for me, no matter how big the ask.

"They're in the office," I told him, gesturing down the hall.

"Want to give me a debrief before I get in there?" he asked, leading the way.

I exhaled, nodded, keeping pace with him. "I looked out the back window, saw a person out there. Didn't realize it was Annie until I got to her. She'd apparently walked from her house"—which was on the other side of the fucking canyon—"in her bare feet and nightgown."

"Jesus Christ," my dad muttered. "Is she okay?"

"Chilled and cuts all over her. I don't know how she made it here in the dark. She didn't have her phone or a flashlight, but she managed to hold on to this the entire way."

We'd reached the door to the office.

My dad turned to me, lifted his brows.

I held up the flash drive.

"What's that?"

"She says it's evidence of Rosie's dad's corruption."

Those brows lifted higher. "What's really on it?"

"No clue," I muttered. "I figured it was best not to open it unless a lawyer was present."

My dad's mouth ticked up into a small smile. "Glad I raised a smart son."

"Sometimes."

He reached for the doorknob. "Is she okay?"

"Annie?" I asked. "Or Rosie?"

"Both of them."

"Annie's slipped back into that fog. I might as well be talking to a piece of furniture for all I get back from her, and Rosie hasn't had much more success."

My dad sighed, shook his head. "And Rosie?"

"Bruised and cut up and bewildered, but taking it like she always does when she gets another blow to the chin." I clenched my teeth, released them. "She just straightens her shoulders and moves forward, ready to take on the fucking world."

He dropped his hand from the knob, brought it to the back of my neck and drew my forehead to his. "We're going to figure this shit out, and she's never going to have to deal with this shit again, never going to have to deal with the world trying to burn her down or tear her to pieces. Okay?"

That fire was burning in my belly, had been for months now.

That my dad was willing to step into those flames with me meant everything.

"Okay," I whispered.

One more squeeze and then he released the back of my neck.

Reached for the knob again.

He pushed the lever, opened the door. Rosie was still standing where I'd left her, taking up position next to the chair her mom was sitting in, where her mom was just staring blankly at the wall.

Rosie moved toward us.

And I saw that same fire burning in her belly.

The Mayoral Magic—no, the Billie Rose Magic. Ready to take on the world, ready to kick ass, even with a cut on her cheek and a black eye.

"Rob," she said, moving in and hugging my dad. "Thanks for yesterday." A breath. "And thanks for being here today."

Business.

All business.

That was okay.

I got it.

Because it was a fuck of a lot better than the bleakness in her eyes from the night before.

She needed those walls, needed that intensity and fire and the rage at what happened to her.

A battle lay ahead of us—

And I had the feeling that we would all need every bit of strength to win it.

SEVEN

BILLIE ROSE

I plugged the flash drive into my computer, keeping one eye on my mother, but knowing she was so off in Never Never Land that she wasn't going to be moving from that chair.

The drive appeared on my screen and I felt my pulse pick up its pace as I clicked it.

As the folders opened and the files appeared.

Audio and pdfs and jpegs and videos.

I glanced up at Rob, who nodded back. So I clicked on the first file, which was a video.

Of me.

I gasped, worry gathering in my belly, and hit the volume, turning it up.

Even though I already remembered exactly when that video had been taken.

It was during a tense meeting with the vice mayor, when I wouldn't sign off on a funding initiative, and—

"That's not going to work," I heard myself say on the video, watching as I set the proposal he'd wanted me to approve to the side of my desk. "You know we have to get approval by the city council. They would be the ones to sign off on something like this."

He began to argue.

But I knew it wouldn't last much longer. He'd get frustrated and leave, and since it was late and I was beyond tired with the bullshit of the day, I would leave too.

But the video wasn't complete.

It had a lot of time left in the file.

So I watched and fast-forwarded through the feed of my empty office.

Until my dad walked in.

Until he reached for that stack of papers, flipped through them.

Then pulled a pen out of the holder, signed across the bottom.

"What did he sign?" Rob asked as he carried them out of the room.

"Approval of funding for a construction company—road work for the far side of town."

Rob nodded, glanced at the screen. "Is the time stamp accurate?"

I squinted, made out the numbers, then pulled out my planner, flipping to that same date, and...there it was. My meeting with the vice mayor. "Yes," I whispered, turning the planner, showing him the entry.

He made more notes.

We went through more videos—saw more papers being signed, saw my father making himself at home in my office, saw him typing on my computer.

"We need copies of those filings," Rob muttered.

I nodded. And we need the planner I had in my office when I was arrested. When the police chief and city attorney showed up, I'd been noting inconsistencies with our files on the cloud, files I knew I hadn't accessed or wasn't in the office to be *able* to access. I didn't bring that with me.

"I'll make sure we get it," he said softly as Joel reached past me and clicked on a jpeg.

"That's the photo Phoebe"—my former archnemesis and the woman brought in to audit me and the department and the city's finances several weeks ago—"sent me of Roger Styles."

"Roger Styles being your dad."

I nodded.

"She grew up in town, right?"

Another nod.

"So why didn't she know who your father was."

I frowned.

"Certainly she would have seen him around town, or at least know who the mayor was."

"Yes," I said. "But she'd never met Roger in person. He was new to the board and missed the day they took pictures. Apparently, Phoebe's assistant had to track him down and tighten a few screws in order to get him to meet the photographer for a makeup session while Phoebe was up here in River's Bend."

Rob nodded, made some more notes, then clicked on another picture.

This one was of my father and Willow—Joel's ex-wife...

Who'd turned out not to actually be an ex.

Because she'd deceived him and hadn't followed up on the paperwork and then Joel had been traded and the fire had happened and...he'd never followed up.

Until she'd shown up in River's Bend.

With instructions from my father to find evidence of my wrongdoing.

And then, later, with instructions to *leave* that evidence.

Piece by piece by piece, my father was erecting a case against me.

But...why?

He'd pushed me to be mayor, pushed me to take on the job when he'd retired. Why would he want to take me down for actually doing it?

Joel clicked another file, this time a PDF, and when it loaded, I began to understand a bit more.

Because this file wasn't from my tenure as mayor.

It was from his.

"Your father didn't start the fire that burned down the town." We all jumped at the sound of my mother's voice. "But he was glad for it."

Rob was the first to recover. "What are you saying, Annie?"

Blankness invading her features.

"Mom," I said sharply, drawing her focus back to mine. "What are you saying?"

"Your father didn't stop being mayor because he got to be old. He stepped down from the position because his lies were getting too big to contain."

I inhaled.

Exhaled.

Waited.

And for once in my life, my mother didn't disappoint me.

"He took kickbacks and hired contractors that did things for him—our pool for free"—she pointed to the monitor—"there's a recording on there," she whispered. "I made it of the two of them —the pool contractor and your father—talking. He threatened to report your father unless the contract for the new city pool went to his company."

Oh my God.

"And there are more conversations," she went on, so fucking quietly I had to strain to hear her. "He never really notices me. And...when I realized what he was doing, I started keeping track, recording on my phone, taking pictures when I could. The files"— a shake of her head—"a lot of the copies I made were burned in the fire, but some of them I managed to save, and I can give them to you..." Her eyes came to mine. "He was watching that feed of you a lot. He saw the arrest, saw the photograph of him on the screen of your computer. He's...I don't know what he's going to do."

Joel's hand came to my shoulder, squeezed lightly.

"I knew I had to get to you, to let you know, to—"

Her throat worked.

"I wasn't a good mother to you," she whispered. "I know that. But I thought—with this—I thought that maybe I could be better."

A tear slid down her cheek.

My head was spinning, digesting, a thousand more questions bouncing around my mind, but none of them actually collating into anything.

"And I-I—" More tears began streaming down her face, her lungs hitched. "He left to go fishing this morning and I knew I had to get out, but you know how he is and I don't drive and—"

And that was the last bit of coherence she gave me.

Sobs wrenched through her, and her legs gave way.

Joel caught her before she hit the floor—because of course he did—lifting her up into his arms, meeting my eyes.

"Guest room," I murmured.

A nod and then he was carrying her from my office and down the hall, settling her into the bed.

She curled up into a ball when I tucked the covers over her.

And maybe I should have sat next to her, tugged her into my arms, maybe I should have held her while she cried.

But...she'd never held me.

This turned out to be a mistake, one I'd seriously regret.

Right then, though, I was focused on other things—the flash drive, the files, my mother...giving me something she never had before.

Right *then*, I was focused on something even more important than that particular mindfuck.

I moved to the bedroom, snagged my cell off the charger.

And I called Dave.

The police chief picked up on the second ring. "Billie, I really can't talk to you—"

"If you ever trusted me, ever thought that I was good at my job, ever thought I valued River's Bend over myself, then I need you to do one thing for me."

A long pause. "What's that?"

"I need you to arrest my father."

EIGHT

"Does your woman like to play with handcuffs in the bedroom too?"

I'd been on the ice less than a minute.

It was still warm-ups.

I couldn't skate over the red line and knock the little shit to the ice, couldn't pummel him and teach him a lesson.

Not yet, anyway.

But it had been three days since my Rosie's world exploded.

The coverage of the "Fallen Mayor" was wide and unrelenting.

So, it was no surprise this asshole was trying to dish it out on the ice.

I still wanted to stab the fucker with my skate though.

"Ignore him," Fox, my teammate who was battling for lumbersexual bachelor of the year with his bushy ass beard and pregame plaid suits, muttered. "You need to focus on the game."

He was right.

If we won this one, we'd be off to the next round.

And I wanted nothing more than to send that little fucker on the other team packing.

End their season.

Let them get a head start on their golf game.

While we kept going.

While we moved on to our battle for the Calder Cup.

We had the team to do it this season.

But I was tired.

I wanted to be back at my house, sitting with Rosie, with our former teammate—and now official NHLer—Axel, his wife, Bailey, who was my Rosie's niece (though they only had two years between them). I wanted to be with my parents, with Dessie, closing ranks around Rosie, making her feel safe and protected and not alone.

I wanted to be keeping an eye on Annie, who may have given her daughter the key to her innocence, but who—frankly—I didn't trust.

Not after she'd spent a lifetime neglecting her daughter, making her feel unworthy of love.

Like Rosie was never enough—never good enough, never working hard enough, a poor replacement for her deceased brother.

I wanted to be going through Rosie's planners and that flash drive with my dad and the rest of them, wanted to be there when Phoebe and Dave, the police chief, came by.

But...hockey.

My team relying on me.

Rosie ill-content to let me avoid my responsibilities.

And...I'd left them once and they won. Now I needed to be here, doing my part, pulling my weight—

"Are those cuffs fur-lined?" the little shit called.

"I'm going to put him through the glass," I muttered, clenching my hands around my stick, probably cracking the composite of fiberglass and carbon fiber.

But I didn't skate across the ice and kill the motherfucker, so that was a victory.

"We're all going to put him through the glass," Fox said.

"All of us. All fucking night," Ryan, another teammate, said, his tone deadly.

Not a surprise.

I was protective, but Ryan took that to an extreme.

And suddenly, I felt better.

Because I wasn't fucking alone. Because my Rosie was surrounded and protected, and because these guys had my back.

Because I was going to take every fucking opportunity to blast that motherfucker.

Boom!

The noise echoed through the arena, boards shaking, glass swaying, the crowd's collective "*Oh!*" trailing shortly after.

Fox following through on his promise earlier.

To crush that motherfucker.

But I was focused right then.

So, it didn't matter.

Because I was already moving, scooping up the puck, tearing up the left side of the ice, carrying it over the blue line.

The defender was flat-footed, a little slow, giving me way too much space.

Clearly, they thought I was going to pass.

And normally, I would have. I was a generous player with good game sense, and my shot wasn't my strongest asset.

I was a passer, a playmaker.

I preferred it that way.

Today, though, I was fucking pissed.

And that D was giving me space to move into the offensive zone, to streak toward the net, to cut toward the center.

So, I was taking it *all* the way in.

I held the puck on my forehead, strode forward once, twice more.

Lifted my stick to fake a shot.

Then rode my edges hard to the right—

A sharp turn to the left, drawing the puck between my legs, tipping it off my skate.

The goalie was still following my stick, still sliding to the right, still trying to recover from my cut back to the left.

Too late.

The puck bounced forward off my skate, exactly where I'd practiced it a hundred, a thousand times before.

Skate to...stick.

A flick of my wrist and the puck was in the back of the net.

Silence for a single heartbeat.

Then the red light flashed on and the crowd erupted.

I slid to a stop, braced because—

Yup.

There it was. My breath being sent out of me in a rush as my teammates closed in, wrapping their arms around me, hugging me and smacking me on the back, sending me crashing into the boards, to the glass, a chorus of "Fuck yeahs!" filling my ears.

I looked through the mess of arms and bodies, sticks and gloved hands, and saw that little shit from earlier still peeling himself up off the ice.

And I smiled.

NINE

ROSIE

I froze, my pen clenched tightly in my hand as I watched Joel snag the puck and start skating hard toward the goal.

"Go," Axel muttered from next to me, gaze glued to the TV. "Fucking *go!*"

I leaned forward, watching the play almost as if it were happening in slow motion—even though it couldn't have been more than a few seconds.

But it was as though my brain knew this was going to be good, going to be important, so it slowed down everything I was taking in—Joel on the TV skating smooth and quick, Axel tense and focused, anticipatory next to me, Rob the legal pad he'd been writing furiously on all day, filling page after page after page, forgotten in his lap.

Dessie clenching her bottle of beer, lips pressed flat.

Bailey whispering, "Come on. Come on. Come *on.*"

"I can't do this," my mom murmured, pushing off the couch and moving out of the room. "I can't sit here and—" A shake of her head before she disappeared.

Frankly, it was a miracle she'd lasted as long as she had, sitting quietly with us in borrowed clothes.

She'd slept all day yesterday.

Had barely come out of the guest room, had barely spoken another word, eaten a bite.

So, that she'd made it through half the game, sitting amongst my friends—not really welcome because...history, but also not excluded because she was my mom—was a miracle.

But she'd stuck through that tenseness.

And now she was out.

Yeah, well, that was a familiar feeling.

My attention went back to the TV, back to my man.

He was beautifully impressive, moving like that, in total control in a way that had my pussy convulsing in memory of all the ways he liked to control, all the ways I was desperate for him to exert that control.

"Oh shit!" Axel said as Joel closed in on the other team's goalie.

And I felt *that* in my bones.

Because my man, my big, strong, and *smooth* man had just executed a move that was dirty as hell—in the best possible way.

And then just casually tapped the puck home, a la Billy Madison and "Go to your home."

Except without the missing.

We all jumped to our feet, high-fived, and for a second, I forgot about my life falling apart, those handcuffs tightening around my wrists. I forgot about everything except Joel and my pride for him and how much I loved him and—

I watched him smile.

Felt my heart jump in my chest.

Because that smile...

It settled in my soul.

And it told me that everything was going to be okay.

———

The knock at the door a couple of hours later had Rob indicating to me to stay seated. "I'll get it."

Dessie had gone home.

Bailey and Axel had returned to their ranch on the far side of River's Bend.

My mom hadn't emerged from the guest bedroom since her mid-game hiatus.

And Joel wasn't yet home from the game.

So, Rob and I were back to yellow legal pads and paper planners, respectively.

Putting everything together.

Helping me clear my name.

"Billie."

I looked up from my planner, saw Dave walking toward me. I hadn't heard a word from him after that phone call the day before, and maybe that was why it wasn't a relief to see him now.

Because I didn't know if he was here to slap cuffs on me again or if he'd come because he'd slapped them on my dad. Because I didn't know if he was here because he believed in me enough to listen or if he...didn't.

"Sorry it took me so long to come over," he said, interrupting my spiral and leaning in to press a kiss to my cheek. "I didn't want any of the media to see me showing up here and kick things off again."

The coverage of my arrest had been brutal.

And the subsequent chaos in Joel's front yard had been intense, was just beginning to die down.

Hope blossomed in my belly.

His voice didn't sound condemning or disbelieving, and he'd been trying to be careful with the press.

That was...nice.

And hope-inducing.

"Oh," I whispered. "Right. Thanks."

He sat on the couch next to me, expression softer than I'd ever seen it.

But I *had* seen that same softness from everyone around me the last few days. Probably because I'd been slowly dying every time I saw a comment or a headline or if one of my friends looked at me like that—like I was fragile and breakable.

Dessie had even taken my phone.

So, I had my planners and my washi...and not one fucking thing to schedule.

No packed agenda.

Nothing to distract myself with.

Just hurt and worry and going through the flash drive and staring at the copies of the public papers we'd downloaded from the public databases. I had a growing list of evidence for my defense and because Rob's paralegals had managed to get some of my personal belongings that had been seized from my office, I also had my planner.

Which had an important page inside it—the list of time stamps I'd been making of files someone had been accessing under my login.

One only three people had—me, my assistant, Bella, and...

My dad.

Paired with everything else, I thought it was pretty clear that I hadn't done what they said I did.

But whether or not anyone would *believe* that, I didn't know.

"So," Dave said. "About your call..."

I tensed, glanced at Rob, holding my breath.

"Your dad's in custody," Dave told me bluntly. "It took a while to track him down, because he wasn't at his normal fishing spot, and because he didn't go back home afterward."

My brows rose. "He didn't?"

Dave shook his head. "I had to track him down two counties over, and his car was full of belongings, Billie. And enough cash to keep him on the road for a while."

My mouth dropped open.

"I think it's pretty fucking clear that there's more going on here than we thought." He pulled out a pad of paper, a pen, flipped to a blank page, then looked up at me expectantly. "So...I'm here to listen."

Relief rushed through me so heavily that my hands started shaking and I had to put my own pen down.

Because he believed in me enough to stick his neck out for me.

Because he believed in me enough to go after my father just because I'd asked him to.

Because...now I could show him.

Now I could prove myself, could get myself out of this mess, could—

"Before we disclose to you what we have," Rob said, sitting on my other side, hand coming to mine and gently cupping it. He was Joel's dad, of course he'd see me shaking. Of course he'd do something about it. "I need you to know that we've made copies of all of this information we're about to share and will be providing it to the city prosecutor and asking her to immediately drop the charges." A beat. "We'll also be releasing this information publicly."

Dave's brows had risen as Rob spoke. But the last had them snapping down, tone going sharp. "I think I already proved that I trust Billie enough to go out on a limb and spend two fucking days looking for—and then quietly arresting—her father without any clear indication of what charges we could press."

My lungs loosened.

"Release the information to who you want to, talk to the prosecutor, put the office on blast," he said. "But know that we went into this fucking reticent as hell, and conducted the investigation as by the book as possible, with the information we were provided and what we were able to collect."

Provided?

But I didn't get a chance to question that because he clicked his pen. "Now, why don't you start at the beginning and tell me exactly what's happening?"

I glanced at Rob.

He nodded.

So...I reached for my laptop, opened it, and...

I played the first file.

———

"Jesus Christ, Billie," Dave muttered, up and on his feet, pacing back and forth.

He had his cell phone out, but no calls actually made yet. Probably because he was alternating between unlocking the screen and then locking it again, tapping the hard-shelled case against his forehead.

"Jesus fucking Christ."

"I don't have everything yet," I told him softly. "There are other inconsistencies we're looking in to, but I think we have enough to prove I didn't do what they said I did."

"We had evidence. We fucking had evidence," he said, whipping toward me. "It felt fucking wrong to look at you that way. You're *Billie Rose*. You live and breathe for River's Bend, and it all felt fucking wrong to sign off on the investigation, to turn over the reports. But, fuck, we *had* evidence—"

I pushed up from the cushions, moved toward him, squeezed his hand. "It's okay. I..." A breath. "I didn't see it at first either. I thought I was going crazy, but then Phoebe mentioned a man from the board of her auditing company"—my childhood enemy and now sort-of friend had been strong-armed by her board to conduct an audit of the city's finances, and that effort had been driven by a man we now knew was my father working under an assumed name—"Roger Styles," I said. "He hired Willow"—Joel's not so ex-wife—"and he pushed going after the audit, forcing Phoebe to take the lead. And I'd just discovered that someone *also* named Roger Styles put in the complaints, started the petition, and filed the recall."

More brow raising from Dave.

"Then just before you arrested me"—a wince, but I pressed on —"Phoebe sent me a picture of Roger Styles." A beat. "It was a picture of my father."

He exhaled. "Jesus fucking Christ."

"Which begs the question of why Rosie's father was trying to implicate his daughter," Rob said. "And what else he might be involved in."

"We found cash," Dave murmured. "And files linking you to money laundering." He glanced up at me. "Specifically to laundering the funding we got after the fire and putting it in your own pocket."

Horror in my gut.

I knew Rob had the full list of charges, but he hadn't given me specifics, and I hadn't asked.

Maybe it was cowardly.

But...I knew it would break me if I knew how far these people thought I'd fallen, how bad they thought I was at my core.

After working so fucking hard, sacrificing so much...

I *couldn't* know it.

Breathe. Think. *Calm.*

"Earlier, you said evidence was provided."

"There was an anonymous drop-off at my house," he said softly. "With files and a note. That started everything. And then we found money here"—a jerk of his chin toward the kitchen counter —"in the baskets you had there."

I frowned because I didn't have baskets—

Only we *did*.

Because my parents had delivered a housewarming basket.

One I hadn't gotten around to unpacking because I was too busy with—you know—my life slowly unraveling.

We hadn't even finished the cookies.

"Your mom," Rob whispered.

"What?"

"Your dad didn't want to be here. He was pissed the entire time. But your mom"—his eyes came to mine—"she was determined to leave it."

My heart convulsed.

My gaze shot down the hall.

Then I was rushing to the guest bedroom, pushing through the door—

And finding...

The bed empty.

And my mom gone.

Ten

JOEL

"Every media outlet on the planet wants to talk about your woman." Coach had drawn me to a halt just inside the door to the locker room, leaning in to speak over the din of my teammates.

"Fuck," I muttered.

"I'll keep them out until you're gone," he told me. "But do me a favor and change quick then get the fuck out of here, yeah?"

"Yeah," I said, still muttering.

Tired as fuck of this shit.

Already hating this shit.

And we were two days in.

But also knowing there was nothing to do but endure it.

So, I nodded my thanks, hustled to my stall, and got out of my gear—sweater into the bin in the center of the room, along with socks and underthings. Helmet, gloves, skates, elbow and shin guards, shoulder pads, jock. All hung up or shoved onto the shelves. The fuck out of the way so I could take the fastest shower on record and get dressed.

Coach nodded at me when I shrugged into my suit jacket, allowing me to slip by him and make my way down the hall toward the exit that led to the player's parking lot.

I turned the corner, bypassing any risk of running into the media...

But nearly running into Fox.

I'd been in such a hurry I hadn't noticed my teammate wasn't in the locker room.

Instead, he was still geared up...

And standing about two inches from Dessie, towering over her, expression fierce, snapping out, "Don't you fucking dare deny that what we—"

Dessie noticed me, probably because I was very much *not* gracefully avoiding the contact, arms windmilling as I did my best to skid to a halt and not interrupt...

Whatever the fuck was going on here.

Because Dessie and Fox were oil and water, and they did not get along, and did *not* like each other at all—

Hmm.

Then again neither had my Rosie and I.

Fox clearly noticed Dessie's reaction because he spun to face me, jerking Dessie behind him, and she wasn't a small woman by any means.

But Fox was a big fucking man.

Her tucked behind him?

She disappeared.

"What the fuck is your problem?" she hissed, shoving at Fox, stepping to the side.

"I thought you were with Rosie," I said, trying to break some of the tense silence that was filling the hallway.

"We called it a night. I just needed to..." Her eyes cut to the side, to Fox, and it was at that moment she seemed to regret being out from behind him, being back on the conversational radar.

"Yeah, sugar lips," Fox muttered, lifting a sardonic brow. "You needed to do what?"

My brows shot up.

He leaned a shoulder against the wall, crossed one skate over the other, taunting grin twisting his mouth. "No quick answer to that, darlin'?"

"Fuck you, Fox," she snapped then shifted her focus back to me. "I was stopping by here to…"

Here she faltered again.

But only for a moment.

Had to give the woman credit—she had spine and could bull-shit with the best of them.

"The media were gone from your house," she whispered. "I wanted to see if they were here instead. I wasn't sure if you'd need someone to run interference or warn you if they were camping out in the parking lot." She nibbled at her bottom lip. "I know Billie was worried, so I decided it was easier to just stop by."

"And you just happened to get back *here*, sugar lips?" Fox murmured, ankles still crossed, sarcasm held in place. "In the player's only section."

"It's not players only," she whispered. "There are staff here too," she added when Fox snorted disbelievingly. "And Timmy let me back when I said I needed to talk to you." This was paired with her glancing at me again.

But I hadn't missed that she'd shifted closer to Fox again, that his body had rotated toward hers.

That neither of them were focused on me.

Not really.

Hmm.

And as interesting as this all was, I didn't want to play this game. I wanted to be home with my woman.

"That's not why you came," Fox said, uncrossing his feet and straightening to his full height. Which—even though I wasn't small by any means—was quite formidable. "Admit it."

Dessie straightened to *her* full height.

Which—considering that she used to be a firefighter before she returned to River's Bend and took over one of the local bars, Monroe's—was formidable in of itself.

"It's none of your business why I'm here," she snapped.

A bushy brow lifted. "It's not?"

Dessie plunked her hands onto her hips, eyes narrowed. "It's not. I'm here because I need to talk to Joel—"

"About the media?" Fox said with a laugh, and hell, if I didn't detect a hint of jealousy in that question.

And seriously, as amusing as this whole scene was, as intriguing as what it hinted at, I just wanted to get the fuck back to my Rosie.

"Dessie," I said firmly enough to draw her focus. "What'd you want to talk to me about?"

Her eyes slanted to Fox then back to mine.

And I got it then.

The web of bullshit she was spinning to protect herself.

Since I'd been spinning my own particular brand of bullshit not all that long ago and not wanting to believe it was bullshit, too fucking scared to admit it was more, I decided to end this, to put her out of her misery.

Because it was a kindness.

Because the sooner I did, the sooner I could get back to Rosie.

"I—" she whispered.

Fox snorted.

But before he could say anything further, voices grew louder in the hall.

"I think I saw him go this way."

"Hurry up."

"*Move out of my way!*"

"I fucking saw him leave first. I get to ask—"

Fox scowled. "Get out of here," he growled. "And take her"—a narrow-eyed glare at Dessie—"with you."

I didn't argue.

Not when I wanted to get home to my Rosie.

Not when I wanted to get the fuck away from whoever wanted to ask me questions about shit I wasn't prepared to answer.

Not when Dessie looked as desperate to escape as I was.

"Come on," I said, taking her arm, drawing her down the hall and toward that back door. "Let's get out of here."

I pushed at the handle, a sliver of night air hitting my face.

"Joel—"

I glanced back at Fox.

He cut his eyes toward Dessie. "Make sure she gets home safe."

I nodded, shoved the door further open, dropped my hand to her back, guiding her outside.

Toward my car.

"I can get home." I slanted a look in her direction, silently telling her to not peddle that bullshit in my direction. "I'm four blocks away," she said, shoulders straightening, chin lifting. "You don't have to drive me. I can—"

I tugged open the passenger's side door of my car, waited.

She sighed, dropped her head back, gaze on the dark sky overhead for one long moment.

Then she exhaled again, brought her chin down...

And got in my car.

I drove her back to Monroe's, to the apartment she lived in above the bar.

Then I took the winding roads.

Back to where I needed to be.

To my Rosie.

Eleven

ROSIE

I spun slowly to face Dave and Rob, who'd followed me down the hall, stomach churning.

"Want to fill me in?" Dave asked quietly.

"I mentioned that my mom showed up yesterday morning." He nodded. "She was supposed to stay here while we sorted everything out."

His gaze flicked around the empty room then back to mine. "And now she's gone?"

"Yeah." I glanced at Rob. "It's just...the basket, the flash drive, the files implicating my dad, and..."

"And now she's gone," Dave said again.

"Yeah."

"Okay," Rob said. "Let's try not to jump to conclusions."

I knew he was right.

Yet I couldn't help but think that I was finally starting to understand the pieces that were moving and shifting behind the scenes, the shit that was trying to close in on me, the people who had rolled the giant boulder to the edge of a cliff and pushed it down the hill, sending it barreling down on me.

People being...my parents.

But was it my mom, my dad, or some awful combination of both?

Had my mom realized the police chief was here, panicked and ran off?

Or had she left because she was part of something more sinister?

A basket with cash and evidence that I was doing something wrong. A camera in my office. Recordings on a flash drive that implicated my dad and not her.

A lifetime of neglect and distance.

A lifetime of standing by as my dad made me feel like I was never enough.

Like I never measured up to a brother who'd died before I was born, whose legacy I could never live up to.

"We'll track her down," Dave said softly. "Work on getting some answers. But I think"—he tucked an arm around my shoulders, drew me out of the room and back down the hall—"that you should let Rob and I speak with the city attorney and prosecutor. We can run with this and put the rest of the shit together."

I glanced at Rob.

His expression was somber, but he nodded.

"Take a few long overdue vacation days," Dave said, squeezing my shoulders. "Watch your man play hockey. And give me and the guys a chance to figure this out."

"*You* and the guys who arrested me," I said tartly. And yeah, maybe that wasn't the smartest—to sass a powerful man who was trying to help me. But *vacation days*? Really? "I should what?" I snapped. "Sit back and let the big, strong men handle it for me? The same ones who fucked it up in the first place?"

That wasn't exactly fair.

I knew it.

But, Jesus fuck, I'd been hauled off in handcuffs all of forty-eight hours before.

By this man.

And we'd grown up together, went to school all the way through twelfth grade together, worked our asses off to rebuild River's Bend.

And he'd still hauled me away in handcuffs without ever talking to me.

Something shifted in my chest. The fracture in my heart enlarging, deepening.

But my attitude wasn't helping figure this out.

"I'm sorry," I said softly.

He squeezed my shoulders again, let me go. "I get it, Billie." A wince. "And I deserve it."

"I appreciate you listening, and being willing to run with this." I glanced down at my feet, clad in a pair of Joel's thick and cozy socks. "I appreciate you believing me yesterday," I whispered.

It was a whisper.

But my fucking voice broke.

He cursed.

Then he was giving me another tight squeeze. "I'm sorry," he muttered. "I should have—"

"I'd appreciate it if you get your fucking hands off my woman."

I jumped back, head whipping to the side, seeing Joel standing just inside the door to the garage, fucking gorgeous in his suit.

Fucking beautiful in his fury.

"Son," Rob chastised quietly.

But I knew what Joel needed.

And that was me. In his arms. Right fucking then.

So, I moved out of the circle of Dave's, and went to him.

But I didn't get within five feet before he was closing the distance between us, tugging me against him, his mouth coming down on mine, his lips parting mine, his tongue slipping into my mouth.

He kissed me deep and long and hot.

And I was kissing him back, forgetting about Dave, forgetting that his dad was in the room, forgetting everything except for Joel's arms around me and his body pressed to mine and the way his kiss made me feel.

Only when I'd been thoroughly tongue-fucked and my brain turned to mush, did he pull back.

I blinked.

Once. Twice.

His hand cupped my jaw and he tilted my face up, looked deeply into my eyes.

God, he was gorgeous.

God, I loved him so fucking much.

"Mine," he muttered, brushing his lips over my forehead.

Then I was tucked against his side and he was glaring over at Dave. "I think it's time for you to go."

I mentally shook myself, focused back in on shit that was real life and not my man kissing me into oblivion. By the time I managed that, I saw that both Dave and Rob had their coats and shoes on and that Rob was packing up his bag.

He slung it over his shoulder, moved over to me, and kissed the top of my head. "I've got this, Rosie girl."

My heart squeezed.

"Thanks," I whispered.

A small smile. "Take those *vacation days*."

I glared.

His smile grew.

Dave—smartly, considering that Joel was still radiating all sorts of possessiveness next to me—just waved and walked to the front door, calling, "Tomorrow."

Then they were gone—the slight squeak of the door opening

and the quiet click of it closing the only sounds beside their footsteps.

Joel moved into me, herding me back, back, back until I was pressed to the counter.

A quick bend had his hands wrapped around my legs and then he was lifting me up, setting me onto the granite. "Stay," he ordered softly.

I nodded.

Then he was gone again and this time I knew the click that I heard was the lock being engaged.

A few moments later, he was back, picking me up from the counter, carrying me over to the couch, sitting down with me in his lap.

"Do I want to ask about the *vacation days* comment?"

"Dave thinks I should sit back and let the big, strong *men* figure out what's going on."

"Because they did that so fucking well in the first place?"

I threw up my hands. "That's what I said!" I scowled. Then wrinkled my nose. "But he does have a point. It's not like I can waltz into the station and accomplish anything." Another sigh. "And your dad isn't letting this go. I can help out from here. I just..."

He settled his forehead on mine. "Hate not being at the center of things, especially something as important as this."

Well... "Yeah."

"Maybe you can't walk into the police station and take over, but you can still be at the center of stuff here, Rosie baby. You can still protect your future and yourself, and I'll do anything I can to help you."

He was so fucking earnest and wonderful and I knew he wasn't lying.

He'd lay down his life for me.

I'd do the same.

And God, I loved him so much.

I cupped his cheeks, fingers sinking into the thick beard there. "You're the only person who wouldn't give me a hard time about being such a control freak, who wouldn't tease me about needing to be at the center of everything."

"Because I know you, and they don't." He drew me closer. "I know it's not ego. It's not even about control." His lips brushed mine. "It's because you care."

My tears stung. "Honey," I rasped.

"And I fucking missed you tonight, Rosie baby," he rasped, burying his face in my hair, arms wrapped tight. "I don't like it when you're not in the stands."

"I know." I curled into his chest. "It sucks watching hockey on TV." I sighed. "I'm sorry I couldn't be there."

A rough laugh. "You're seriously apologizing after the last couple of days?"

I shrugged. "It hasn't been easy for you either," I murmured. "And you missed a game, had to play tonight knowing all this shit was happening and—*ack!*"

Suddenly, I found myself on my back, his big body pressing me into the couch cushions. "That's the last fucking time you'll apologize, sweetheart. We're in this together. We love each other. When we're in the shit, we're *both* in the shit."

I scowled.

Because that was exactly what I didn't want—my shit bleeding over into his shit.

Even as I knew he was right.

I'd never hesitated to help people solve their problems, to help Joel with his.

But it was a fuck ton lot harder to accept that same from him in return.

Yet...I knew he needed me to be able to do that.

Knew he needed to look after me, same as I did for him.

"You're right," I told him, clocking that his expression immediately changed, immediately relaxed, immediately softened, those deep green eyes of his going gentle.

And they stayed gentle as I filled him in about the last few hours—what his dad and I figured out, what Dave had shared and the news about my dad being in custody.

About my mom going AWOL and what that might implicate about her involvement in the shitstorm surrounding me.

"Jesus, Rosie baby," he muttered. "That was a busy few hours."

"Tell me about it," I muttered back.

He nuzzled at my throat. "We'll figure this out."

I knew *we* would.

Because I had Rob and Dessie and Bailey and Axel and Dave and Fox and—

I had hope.

And determination.

And this man who would protect my heart to his last breath at my side.

"I know."

He studied me closely, brushed his lips over mine. "Good, baby." A half smile as he cupped my jaw again and I felt the tension melt away. Felt it morph into something different. Because his gentle green eyes began to flicker with heat, emeralds with sparks of flames. "You know," he murmured. "There is *one* good thing about the guest room being empty..."

My brows lifted, but already curls of need began to coil in my belly. "Oh yeah?"

He nuzzled at my neck. A nip of his teeth. "Yeah."

"And what's that?"

TWELVE

JOEL

I slid my hand up her side.
Slipped it beneath her bra.
Cupped one lush breast. "This, Rosie baby."

She hissed out a breath, lids going half-mast, lips parting on a shaking exhale. "Are you—" She broke off, nibbled at her bottom lip. "Aren't you tired?"

"No."

Those teeth slipping free of that lip, concern sliding into blue eyes. Her expression going soft in a way that she only ever gave me. "Oh."

I let more of my weight sink into her, let her feel exactly how *not* tired I was.

Another hissed-out breath.

Her blue eyes going molten.

"Yeah." I nipped at her bottom lip. "*Oh.*"

She shuddered, hands diving into my hair, hips arching beneath mine. "I'm scared," she whispered.

That had my desire freezing, and I rolled to my side, drawing her against me. "I know, Rosie baby. But I'm here, and we're together, and I promise you, it will be okay."

She exhaled, head dropping to my collarbone, breath on my skin. "How do you know it will be okay?"

"Because you're incredible, sweetheart," I said, winding my hand into her hair, tilting her head back, brushing my lips over hers. "Because you've survived a nightmare and thrived. Because we survived a fire and we're stronger for it. Because you're Billie Fucking Rose, the kickass mayor of River's Bend, and you've never met a crisis or a problem you couldn't solve." I cupped the side of her neck. "Never, Rosie baby. And that's not going to change with this bullshit, okay?"

Her eyes glimmered with tears, but she nodded, whispered, "Okay."

I smoothed my hand over her hair, the curls dancing over my fingers. "I love you."

A sigh, her lips pressing to my throat. "I know."

I sank my fingers into her curls, tugged lightly. "Rude."

She shivered...

And I learned something new about my woman, rolling us so she was beneath me again, so those heated eyes were on me again. "You like that," I murmured.

She could have demurred.

But my Rosie was a straight shooter.

And she wasn't shy in the bedroom.

"I like that," she said, arching against me. "And I'd like it a fuck of a lot better if we were both naked and you were pounding into me from behind while you did it."

My dick went hard.

"Rosie," I rasped.

She grinned up at me.

Then she did what she always did—she kicked some ass.

In this case, *my* ass.

Sliding a hand down between us, reaching for the button on

my slacks, flicking it open. She didn't tease me as she dragged down the tab of my zipper and plunged her hand inside my pants, my underwear, wrapped her fingers around my cock, squeezing hard enough to make me see stars.

"Christ, baby," I said, thrusting into her hands.

"You like it," she said, nipping at my jaw.

I did like it.

But I liked making her come more.

I pushed off the couch, taking her with me, bringing us to our feet. But my woman was fucking tenacious, and she didn't lose her grip, kept pumping as I shoved her leggings and underwear down.

I ripped her shirt and bra over her head, and that was when I lost her fingers.

That was okay. I had other plans.

Starting with propping her on the back of the couch.

Spreading her legs to put that pretty pussy on display.

Kneeling between her thighs.

"Like the socks, Rosie baby," I murmured, kissing just above her ankle, where the pair of socks she'd stolen from my drawer was bunched.

"They're c-cozy," she stuttered as I trailed my tongue up.

"Mmm." I nipped at the back of her knee, felt her subsequent shudder in my cock. "I think I'm going to make you wear them every time I fuck you."

Another shiver.

I dragged my teeth along her inner thigh, up through the crease at the hinge of her hips, not missing that she widened her legs, that she arched her pelvis.

That she wanted more.

I didn't give it to her, not right then anyway.

I began kissing my way along her other thigh, down toward her ankle.

"How about you fuck me now?"

I wanted that.

I wanted her to forget about everything, to lose herself completely as she came apart on my tongue.

A nip to her other ankle.

"Joel," she demanded, legs widening. "I want you."

The need in her voice had my dick twitching.

But I had a plan.

And I wanted my tongue in her cunt.

I shifted again, leaning closer, making my way back up, slowly, incrementally, knowing it was killing her, that she was getting impatient, if the bite of her nails into my scalp, the tug of my hair was any indication.

Slow. Steady.

That was the plan.

Especially as I watched that pink pussy plump and glisten, all but calling out for my mouth, my teeth, my tongue and fingers and cock.

I could smell the musk of her.

My mouth watered.

But, still, I took my time.

"Honey," she begged when I stopped with my mouth an inch from that pussy, saliva pooling in my mouth, my tongue desperate to taste.

I blew out a stream of air.

She shivered...and then did the best fucking thing ever.

She lost patience, launching herself off the top of the couch. I caught her before her feet hit the floor, tossing her legs over my shoulders, latching onto her clit.

A gasp, her hands coming to my head, my hair, pulling hard enough to send a spike of pain through my scalp.

Best fucking pain of my life.

Because her desire was on my tongue, in my mouth, dripping down my beard.

I straightened and spun, laying her out on the dining room table, like she was the best fucking meal of my life.

And she was as I sucked her clit and thrust a finger inside her, feeling the clamp of that cunt around me, my cock protesting because it wasn't inside too.

"Joel," she groaned, hands still in my hair but this time to hold me still as she ground her pussy against my face. "Fuck, I love your beard."

"Fuck, Rosie baby," I muttered, dangerously close even though I wasn't even inside her yet, wasn't feeling the hot clamp of her. I slid another finger inside her and she groaned again, digging the back of her head into the table, her legs tightening around me.

"Please, honey." Her eyes flashed open, molten sapphires. "Please come inside me."

So fucking pretty.

This cunt.

The pleading in her eyes.

The red on her cheeks, the way her nipples had puckered, all but begging for my mouth and fingers.

"Joel."

My name on her tongue.

I bent, redoubled my focus on her clit, fucked her rough and dirty with my fingers, the slick sounds of her desire, her pleasure filling the air.

I felt the change inside her before I heard it in my ears.

And my control snapped.

THIRTEEN

ROSIE

I felt the change in him even though I was losing my mind, losing myself to the need and desire and pleasure.

That was welling up within me.

Rolling through me in huge, great waves that threatened to sweep me out to sea.

"Oh God," I whispered as he sucked my clit harder, as those fingers fucked me hard and fast and deep.

As I exploded, sparks flashing behind my closed eyes, my body going so fucking tense...and then loose as the pleasure peaked and then slowly ebbed away, millimeter by millimeter by millimeter.

When I finally managed to peel back my lids, it was to see my man rising from between my spread legs, pants unzipped and barely hanging on his hips, underwear out of place from when I'd had my fingers around him earlier. I watched him slowly unbutton his shirt, exposing inch after inch of his gorgeous chest.

Strong pecs that I'd copped many of feel of.

A flat abdomen, faint lines of his muscles visible when he inhaled—something he was doing regularly and rapidly.

A sprinkling of hair on his chest, a thin trail disappearing beneath his underwear.

But his expression was the sexiest thing that I'd ever seen.

His eyes fucking burned as he stared down at me, hands still moving on the buttons of that shirt, then shifting to his pants and underwear. This man was a fucking Viking standing over me, preparing to fuck me. His movements might be deliberate, might hint at a semblance of control.

But I knew him as well as he knew me.

I clocked his hands shaking, the bead of sweat on his temple.

He was on the hair trigger, one second away from losing it.

And I couldn't wait to send him over the edge.

I started to sit up.

His palm hit my chest, pushing me back down. "No."

I shivered—not because I was cold, but because that fierce command pressed right at my clit—something I knew he recognized because he didn't lift me off the table or get a blanket or find a way to warm me, like he would have, if I was truly uncomfortable.

Nope.

He just pressed that warm, rough hand to my front, dragging it down between my breasts, over my stomach, not stopping until he was cupping my pussy, thick fingers sliding through my slick folds.

"Stay," he ordered.

I shivered again.

He grinned down at me, but it wasn't amusing in the least.

It was hot and sinful and...

His pants hit the floor. His cock sprung free. And...fucking *yes*, I needed this man inside me.

Thankfully, he didn't delay.

Gripping my hips and yanking me toward him, yanking me until my ass rested on the edge of the table.

"Honey," I whispered when he swept his fingers over me, teasing my entrance with one blunt fingertip.

He dipped his finger inside.

I shuddered, trying to move closer, to get my elbows beneath me, to lift up and get this fucking man inside me.

He just dropped that hand to the center of my chest again.

Pressed me back down.

"Stay," he ordered again.

Swear to fuck, if a man tried to tell me to *stay* in the real world, I would have eviscerated him. But this man telling me to *stay* with me naked and spread out before him like I was the fucking Last Supper...

It was fucking glorious.

That finger slid in, out, in, out.

In.

One firm thrust.

And then it wasn't his fingers. He was inside me, thick and hard and hot, stretching me to my limits, the burn only adding to my pleasure, my need—

"Fuck, Rosie baby," he groaned, hands back at my hips, pulling me toward him as he thrust up inside me.

Deep.

Rough.

Perfect.

"I love you," I whispered. "But I fucking *love* your cock."

A wolfish smile.

Those hips not stopping, those hands still tight.

I didn't feel the hard surface of the table beneath me, didn't feel the edge of the wood biting into my ass. My senses were reduced to this man and his hands, this man and his rasping voice ordering me to, "Take it, Rosie baby. Take it like the good girl you are."

I gasped when he pressed my legs wider, when he thrust somehow deeper.

He was bumping into the edge of my womb, but somehow, it wasn't too much. Somehow I wanted more, wanted everything.

And he gave it—bending and sucking a nipple in his mouth, his thumb coming to my clit in a double-pronged attack.

All while his hips kept pistoning.

All while he kept talking.

"Such a pretty pussy," he murmured around my flesh, the words vibrating through my already sensitized skin.

I bucked against him.

But he just held me still and. Fucked. Me. So. Damned. Good.

Nipples and clit.

Then stealing my mouth in a kiss that left me dizzy.

My entire body was a sensitized nerve, a bundle of desperation and need.

"Come," he ordered, rhythm faltering for the first time, telling me exactly how close to the edge he was. "Come now, Rosie baby. I want to feel you tighten around my cock."

As if I could stop the flood of pleasure rising within me.

As if I could deny this man anything.

I let go...

And I came apart.

And just like every other time before, Joel caught all of the pieces of me.

And...he put them back together.

———

My cell rang way too early the following morning.

The sun was barely up.

My body felt like it had been ridden hard and put up wet.

And it had, I supposed, Joel's cum dried at the tops of my thighs.

I shivered, remembering the rough and dirty way he'd fucked me.

Remembering how much I'd liked it.

Buzz. Buzz. Buzz. Buzz.

Right.

My phone.

I shimmied to the side, trying to slip out from beneath Joel's heavy arm, which was wrapped tightly around my middle, folded up between my breasts, fingers holding tight to my shoulder.

I loved when he held me like that, loved how secure it made me feel.

Buzz. Buzz. Buzz. Buzz.

"Hello?" I rasped into the receiver.

A long pause.

Then Rob's voice came through. "Shoot, I'm sorry I woke you, Rosie girl."

Rosie girl.

It wasn't Rosie baby.

But it meant something big. Meant a lot to me. Meant that Joel's dad truly accepted me.

Okay, I knew that already.

I just...it meant *something* to me.

"It's okay," I said, sitting up in the bed. "We were up late is all." He made a noise that sounded like it was going to form into an apology, so I hurried to say, "But I'm awake now. What's happening?"

A blip of quiet.

Then, "I need you to come down to the police station."

Fourteen

Joel

"We'd like to issue a public apology to Mayor Donovan and do it as quickly and openly as possible."

The crowd gasped, background noise making it difficult to hear what Dave—the bastard who'd had his hands on my woman when I'd come home from the game the week before—was saying. He was in full police regalia, positioned in front of a plethora of microphones, a bevy of press surrounding him.

"As law enforcement officers, we do our best to always get it right, and in this case, we didn't," he said and turned to my Rosie, who was standing behind the podium, my dad next to her. "I'm sorry."

I watched the apology hit my woman, wished I was at her side instead of states away, playing in the next round of the playoffs.

Hating that I was watching this shit on my phone.

Hating that my job took me away from her.

Again.

She nodded slightly, and I watched my dad squeeze her shoulder, thanked fuck for my family, for Rosie's found family, who I knew were standing in the wings, ready to shelter her, to support and protect her.

I knew I'd be there soon.

Just not as soon as I wanted.

We had our game tonight and then we were jumping on a plane and flying home.

So, I'd be able to hold her tonight—or the middle of it, anyway. I'd be able to tell her how proud I was of her.

But I wasn't there *now*.

I clenched my phone as Dave turned back to the cameras, to the microphones. "We've had more evidence come to light over the last week, and the district attorney will brief the media on that once she is available to do so. For now, this department felt it was important to share the information that all of the charges that had been filed against Mayor Donovan have been dropped."

More crowd noise.

But Dave shook his head. "We won't be taking any questions. Thank you." He spun away from the microphones, moved to my Rosie and shook her hand.

Then they were all walking back into the building, disappearing inside, and the feed was cutting back to a news desk.

"You've heard it here first, folks. Mayor Donovan has been cleared of any involvement in the money laundering scheme in River's Bend. But the question remains, where have those millions of dollars in state emergency funds gone?"

I hit the button on the side of my phone, locking the screen and cutting off the feed.

"That's it then," Fox muttered.

"That's it," I agreed, even if I knew that it wasn't it. They'd come out and cleared my Rosie, but a subset of the population would never hear that retraction, and others wouldn't believe that a mistake had been made.

They would always look at her like she'd done something wrong.

And maybe she'd be able to ignore it.

But she'd know it, she'd feel it, and she'd hate it.

And I had to go out on the ice tonight and focus, knowing that I wasn't with my woman, knowing she was hurting, knowing that even though things were finally looking up, they weren't anywhere near perfect.

I had to go on the ice and play hockey and know it was dividing us.

Again.

———

A few days later, I knocked softly on the doorway to my Rosie's office.

Normally I would have left her to do her thing at work, left her to rock her shit as she always did.

But...it was lunchtime.

But...it was her first day back in the office.

And I couldn't go through my day, looking at the text she'd sent in response to *my* text, the words a reassurance, and yet, not one either.

Because River's Bend was going back to normal.

But my Rosie wasn't.

The recall had been withdrawn—because it turned out that the majority of the signatures on it had been fraudulent.

The petitions were dismissed.

Everyone was business as usual.

Even my Rosie.

But...she wasn't right.

And I was waffling between striving for patience and wanting her to spill her guts, to admit that she was hurting and confused and—

Instead, she'd just buttoned up her crisp white shirt, slipped on a pair of heels I knew she hated, then had kissed me goodbye and walked out the door.

Like it was a normal morning.

When I fucking *knew* it wasn't.

"Hey," she said, eyes flicking to mine, mouth curving up. "Just give me one second." Her gaze went back to the screen, she typed a few things on her keyboard, and then she pushed in the keyboard tray, rolled her chair back, and stood, crossing over to me. "You heading to the rink?"

"I'm taking you to lunch."

Her brows flicked up and her gaze slid to the computer then back to me. "I have a lot of work to do."

"Sweetheart," I admonished quietly. "You know I'm not going to let you get away with that shit."

"I'm mayor again." A shrug. "And I've got a backlog of stuff from when I wasn't working. And I have media and meetings with your dad about the case and I'm still finding errors that only come from me being in this job, knowing the ins and outs." She exhaled. "And my mom is gone."

Back to normal...

And not.

"That doesn't mean she's involved," I pointed out.

Rosie shot me a look that seemed to say, "What else could it mean?" but she didn't say that aloud, just held perfectly still as I brushed the curls out of her face, as I tried not to look at the patched-over hole in the wall in the corner of her office, where Dave and several officers had removed the camera her father—and perhaps, her mother—had used to spy on her.

They'd checked the entire room, searching it from top to bottom.

But had only found the one camera.

That was something.

A *small* something.

But I'd come to understand that we had to take the small somethings too.

"Did Dave give you an update on the recordings?"

The police had run another search of her parents' house and found more monitoring equipment and computers and recordings.

"The hard drives were wiped." She sighed and leaned heavier against me. "So, no footage of my dad doing anything in here." She pressed her lips together, released them. "Or my mom."

"Damn," I muttered.

"I know," she said, dropping her head to my collarbone, her arms coming around my middle. "Though, I suppose that's a good thing, considering the stuff you and I got up to in this office."

I stilled.

Remembering exactly what we'd gotten up to—or what I'd gotten inside.

Guilt slicing ribbons through my insides. "Shit, sweetheart, I didn't—"

She rose up on tiptoe, brushed her mouth over mine. "I'll remind you that I was an active participant in any and all desk fucking." Her gaze flicking to the filled-in part of the wall. "Though, I don't think it's something we'll be repeating, no matter how glorious it was."

I tugged a curl. "That's fair."

A kiss to my jaw.

She turned away, and I wondered if she'd still put me off for lunch.

But she just opened her desk drawer, tugged out her purse, and moved back over to me. "Ready?"

I plucked it out of her hands, dropped it back into the drawer, and slammed it shut.

"Really?" she asked dryly.

"You're not paying," I muttered.

Which—for some reason—made her both smile and shake her head.

Then loop her arm through mine.

"I'm hungry, honey."

FIFTEEN

BILLIE ROSE

"I knew they couldn't be right," Edy murmured, squeezing my hand. "I just knew it."

Yeah?

Well, it certainly hadn't felt that way when she'd blasted me all over Facebook right after the arrest.

But I didn't say that, just smiled and nodded and extricated myself from this conversation.

More abruptly than my father would have ever approved of.

But considering all he'd done, I wasn't bothering to spend much time worrying about how he'd judge me for handling an interaction.

Yay, me.

It only took getting hauled off in handcuffs and stuck in county jail, with my face plastered all over the interwebs and television, and everyone talking about what a terrible person I was, for me to finally realize that my father had no right to judge me.

Meanwhile, he'd been—

Shitting all over every value he'd so painstakingly tried to impart.

And my mom...

Had cut her losses? Had finally decided to put the past behind her? Had taken her chance to move on?

To forget about my dad.

And me.

The last wouldn't be a surprise. She hadn't spent much of her life thinking about me.

But...she also hadn't spent much of her life *living*, and the thought of her suddenly becoming a criminal mastermind was just...

Unfathomable.

Wiring cameras and creating schemes and manipulating my father—*my father*—it seemed impossible.

But then again, she'd filled a flash drive with files that perfectly incriminated my father.

And exonerated me.

So...

I didn't know what to think.

And she wasn't in town, wasn't available for me to ask her, and—

"That good, huh?"

I blinked, realized I'd walked away from that conversation with Edy and pretty much put myself in a corner. Like literally walked into an empty corner, facing said corner, and...

Yeah.

I'd basically put myself in timeout.

I turned to Dessie, shrugged. "It's not the ideal view," I said, going for light.

"Well," she said, stepped close and leaning back against the wall with her arms and ankles crossed, mouth curved up into a smirk. "I can see a sliver of the ice."

I chuckled. "It's not good to feed into your friend's delusions."

She sobered. "I think you've had enough reality for a while, honey."

"Don't," I whispered, eyes stinging.

A long, somber study of my face. Then she sighed and I watched her deliberately shove the seriousness away. "Well, at least your delusions involve a hot hockey player."

I grinned. "Sure you don't want to find your own?"

Pale skin, wide eyes, but another thing deliberately shoved away. Hmm. But before I could pounce on that—and seriously, I was ready to pounce on anything that wasn't me dealing with the shit that had surrounded my life of late—she said, "Yeah, no. I'm not into guys who spend all their spare time playing with their sticks."

I snorted. "Sometimes that stick-playing ends up being a good thing."

Her shoulder bumped against mine. "Dirty, dirty bitch."

I grinned, and it felt real for the first time in a long time. In too long. "Damn right, I am. You know that Joel loves my handcuffs."

"And *that*, Madame Mayor, is far too much information for you to be sharing with me."

Madame Mayor.

All that quick compartmentalization

God, that title burned as it hit my eardrums, as it settled on my shoulders, as it sank barbed claws into my heart.

All I'd ever wanted.

All I'd *never* wanted.

All I didn't want now.

Dessie jerked, all the amusement sliding from her face, concern taking its place. "Rosie," she began.

"Billie Rose!"

Now we both jerked, spinning to see Bella hurrying toward me, the expression on my assistant's face telling me that I had a half dozen fires to put out.

"Just a second, Bells," Dessie said, intercepting her. "I only need another thirty seconds of the mayor's time."

"But—"

"Just a *second*," Dessie semi-repeated, but with more force this time. Then she grabbed my arm, pulled me further into the corner. "Okay, Rosie," she said firmly. "Now is the time that you spill whatever the fuck it was that put that look on your face."

"I forgot about—"

"Bullshit," she said, not even giving me enough time to finish the lie. "And don't try that nonsense again."

I sighed, studied my friend, studied how serious she was.

Deadly serious about not letting my bullshit stand.

"It's..." I sighed. "This is all just messed up and people are staring at me, and others are judging me, and it's all just really raw right now, you know?"

Her head tilted to the side, sleek black ponytail swinging behind her. "I don't know," she said. "I can't know what it's like." Her hand found mine, squeezed. "But I do know what it feels like to have the foundation of my life shaken like it's a magnitude eight point five on the Richter scale, and I know that you need to give yourself some time to find yourself on stable ground again. You can't just expect to jump back in and—"

"Billie!"

Bella's voice was far more urgent and I turned to face her, Dessie following suit. "What's up, Bells?"

"The new sewer downtown ruptured and sewage is flooding Main Street."

I sighed, dropping my head forward, chin hitting my chest.

Then I pulled on my mayor hat—summoned some of what Joel had termed my Mayoral Magic. "Call the head of Public Works."

Bella nodded, already dialing on her phone as she turned and walked away.

I glanced at Dessie, lifted a brow. "And," I said without humor. "I can't just expect to not jump back into that?"

My friend winced. "Okay, Madame Mayor. I'll give you that one."

I tugged out my own phone, mind racing, and started moving toward the exit, crisis mode activated.

"Hey." Dessie moved up next to me, holding the door to the rink open so I could walk through it.

I paused.

She bumped her shoulder against mine. "I'll save you a seat next to the glass."

"Thanks, Des," I murmured, waving as she went back inside then walking quickly toward Bella, who was already outside, focusing on the list of things I would need to do.

Focusing on the work.

Stepping back into this role.

Issuing orders.

Solving another crisis.

And ignoring that everything about this felt wrong.

Sixteen

Joel

She'd made it to the game in the third period, curls a riotous mess that I wanted to dive my fingers into while I fucked her from behind.

Clothes mussed in a way that had my thoughts diverting further from hockey.

When they really should be focused on the game.

But it was her eyes that really had me struggling to concentrate.

The whistle trilled and I jerked to attention, stick settling on the ice, eyes trained on the face-off dot, waiting for Fox to win the puck—because he did so often, it was almost a certainty.

Fucker.

If he wasn't on my team, I'd seriously hate the bastard.

The puck dropped, and he—no surprise—won it over to Ryan.

A quick flick back, sent it to our defenseman at the blue line, who ripped a shot toward the net.

But this was the playoffs. This was professional hockey.

It wasn't that easy.

The goals didn't come easy. The game wasn't *won* easily.

But we did come out on top in the end.

Another game won. One step closer to the Cup.

And all the while, my gaze kept drifting toward the glass, toward my Rosie. Who was doing all the right things—smiling when people spoke to her, nodding regularly, jumping to her feet and cheering when Ryan scored.

But...it was all wrong.

The press was still busier than was typical after one of our games—the extra attention from Rosie's arrest and then her name being cleared still bringing more reporters into the locker room than we usually saw. But it was relatively painless—and more focused on hockey than drama for a change.

So, I could handle it.

What I *couldn't* was walking out of the locker room, freshly showered (and I couldn't lie—those showers would always bring the best fucking memories...of fucking and my Rosie) to find my woman in a crowd of people...

And none of this shit was right.

Her smile. Her eyes. The way she held herself, like she was on the edge and one more push would send her off the cliff, down to the bottom, send her shattering into a million pieces.

All while the crowd of people were surrounding her, closing in like fucking zombies after brains.

"I just knew it," someone was saying. "Knew it couldn't be true."

"Those petitions were a mistake," said another.

Someone clapped her on the back. "Only you could get that sewer main sorted so quickly."

"Any word on the soccer tournament?"

I wrapped my arm around my Rosie's middle, drew her back against me.

The crowd faltered, growing quiet.

"Excuse us," I muttered, seeing more than one set of eyebrows lift, seeing more than one mouth curve into a knowing smile.

I wanted to snarl at them, to tell these people they had no fucking clue what they had put my woman through, what they were doing to her now.

But my Rosie was more important.

What was putting that look on her face was more important.

What was...making her hurt and withdraw and slap on that mayor mask of hers was more important.

I tugged her back, drawing us around the corner and into an empty office we used to review tape in. There was a couch shoved against one wall, so I sat us down on it, tugging her into my lap. "Spill it, Rosie baby."

She frowned up at me. "First, Joel," she muttered, "I don't like it when you manhandle me."

"That's bullshit."

That frown deepened. "Excuse me?"

It was an arch question, a dangerous one, but I ignored it and said, "You fucking love it when I use my strength with you, so don't try to bullshit me."

"Not in front of my constituents," she snapped.

"Those constituents that didn't stop you from dealing with petitions and a recall and trashed you after the arrest?"

Her expression turned stark. "Don't," she whispered.

"Rosie baby," I murmured, gently cupping her jaw. "I need you to talk to me."

"There was a sewer main break downtown," she said softly. "That's why I missed the first two periods. I needed to help Bella coordinate the right resources." A sigh. "It couldn't be a water line that broke. Nope. It has to be raw sewage and a health hazard and —" She closed her eyes, leaned into my palm. "It's never easy, is it?"

"No," I agreed. "But that's not what's really bothering you, sweetheart."

She went still, lids peeling open, those gorgeous blue eyes on mine, holding mine as they swam with pain.

I smoothed my free hand up and down her side.

And waited.

For a long, long time.

"No," she finally admitted. "It's not what's really bothering me."

I waited again.

Even longer.

"You know that I love you, that I'll never judge you, right?"

She went tense, so fucking tense against me, and I knew they were the right words...and simultaneously the wrong ones as well.

But I didn't get the chance to backtrack.

Because she whispered, "I don't want to do this anymore."

My hand stilled on her side, gut clenching,

"I *can't* do this," she went on, still whispering.

What the fuck?

What the *fuck?*

She didn't want to do this, to do *us* anymore?

She *couldn't* do it?

Fuck. That.

I snapped out of my surprise, pushed down my hurt—because I wasn't fucking letting her go—and brought my other hand up, cupping both of her cheeks, panic making my movements jerky, my words come out in a rush. "Rosie baby, we'll figure it out. Work through—"

"I don't want to be mayor."

Relief flooded through me—all that fear and hurt disappearing in a second.

Because our relationship—*me*—wasn't what she was talking about.

But then it was gone a moment later.

Because she didn't want to be *mayor?* That was her. That was my Rosie—all she'd lived for, all she wanted, all that she'd worked so damned hard for.

And also...apparently not.

"Rosie—"

The door swung open and Fox poked his head in. "Joel, man" —his eyes flicked between us—"sorry, Rosie, but we've got to get on the bus."

The bus to the airport.

For our flight that left tonight.

Because we had another fucking game that was going to take me away from my woman.

Fox let the door swing shut as Rosie hopped to her feet, tugging me into a tight hug, a sweet kiss.

"Sweetheart."

She cupped my jaw. "Later."

I opened my mouth to protest, but then she was pulling the door back open, joining the rush of activity in the hallway, tugging me behind her.

Toward the fucking bus.

Onto the fucking bus.

While she remained outside.

But as we drove away, the words didn't stop running through my mind.

Seventeen

Rosie

I'd slept alone in our bed last night.

Which shouldn't have been a relief, but after the look on Joel's face when I'd admitted—

God, I couldn't even believe that I'd admitted it to myself, let alone said it out loud to him.

Which was part of why I was working from home today.

Avoiding the office and the feelings growing in my belly.

Avoiding the truth that was growing heavier by the moment.

That was why I'd gone back downtown after the bus had driven away. Why I'd spent hours in the dark avoiding as I tried to forget about the look on his face.

A combination of shock and horror and—

Disappointment.

Or maybe I was projecting.

I groaned, dropped my head into my hands, leaning forward and resting my elbows on my desk.

Working from home.

Ha.

More like staring at my inbox that was growing by the second and pretending to get shit done.

On that note, I couldn't sit at my desk for a moment longer.

I pushed up to my feet, my chair rolling backward, and grabbed my water bottle. I'd top it off, pretend I was doing something productive.

Drinking those eight glasses of water a day.

Go me!

Shaking my head, I topped off the metal bottle, screwed on the lid, and debated between carrots and a cookie.

But when I remembered they were snickerdoodles—my mom's specialty (though these were store-bought ones that Joel had kindly picked up)—any sugar craving disappeared.

Carrots it was.

I dumped some in a bowl, slopped some hummus in with them.

Yay.

Also, yes, my expression at the healthy snack wasn't pleased.

But since I didn't have a vat of ice cream or the time or energy to make something else, I just picked up my bowl and started to carry it from the kitchen.

Knock. Knock.

Immediately, I went on alert, debating between answering it and turning around, hightailing it to my office, and hiding.

But—dammit—I was Billie Fucking Rose.

I ate chaos for breakfast.

I set down my bowl, moved to the front door, and pulled it open.

But when I saw who was on the other side, I regretted not hiding. Because...

It was Willow.

Joel's gorgeous, put-together, not-so-ex-wife *Willow* with the perfect winged liner and perfect body and perfect face and perfect outfits.

Which, today, was a perfectly paired crisp button-down and slacks, flats, earrings, and a statement necklace.

She looked like she'd walked right out of a stock photo titled Working Woman.

And I...

Well, I'd changed out of my pajama bottoms.

That was the best I had.

"Billie," she said softly as I was wrestling the comparisons away, as I was working equally as hard to put another time when this woman had showed up out of the blue on my doorstep out of my mind.

Chipping away at my happiness.

My world.

My relationship with Joel.

And I didn't know why she was here now.

"Willow," I said, pushing that away. "Can I help you with something?"

"Can I—" She bit her lip, blond hair shining in the sunlight. "Can I come in?"

No. God, I didn't want to deal with this.

But...another day, another thing I didn't deal with. I forced a smile, stepped back. "Of course. Can I get you anything?" I asked after I'd closed the door and led her into the kitchen. "Coffee? Carrots?" I held up my bowl.

Willow blinked. "No," she murmured after a moment. "Thanks."

We stood there staring silently at each other for far longer than I was comfortable with.

"What can I do for you?" I eventually broke down and asked into the taut silence.

Her shoulders rose and fell on a breath, and then she extended her hand, passing over a folder. "I signed the divorce papers."

My mouth dropped open so quickly, my jaw actually ached in protest.

Another breath, her eyes holding mine again. "Our visas came through."

Now my teeth clicked together.

"I have an apartment lined up and I'm going to get my son here, going to get my mom here."

"I—" Here I faltered.

Because this was the best damned news I'd had in ages.

"Are you staying in town?" I asked carefully.

A shake of her head. "No," she murmured. "I'm going back to LA. There are more jobs and it's closer to the doctors who can treat my mom."

"I see," I said carefully, even though inside I was torn between a niggle of worry about her, her mom, and her son in a big city like Los Angeles, and so fucking glad Joel was almost done with her, almost done with this mess.

"I can't keep doing this to you and Joel," she said, making me feel like a dick for that half-mental celebration. "You've both been through enough."

"I—"

She squeezed my hand. "It's done now." She backed away, dropped her arm to her side. "I'm guessing you'll pass the news on to Joel at the right time?"

"Uh...yeah."

Her mouth quirked up, probably because I sounded really fucking eager to do just that.

"I—" I began, but she was already turning for the front door.

She paused and glanced back after she opened it.

"I won't bother you and Joel again. I promise."

Then she stepped outside, shut the wooden panel behind her.

She'd lied before.

But today I believed her.

I flipped through the divorce papers, made a call to Amy— Joel's lawyer and the best family law attorney in River's Bend.

Then I called my man.

"Willow was here," I said when he answered.

A blistering curse.

"No, wait, it's good news, honey."

And then I told him.

And then...I went back to work for the first time since my return with a real smile on my face.

Eighteen

"I need a purple one, Mr. Joel."

I glanced up at the little girl whose bright blue eyes reminded me of my Rosie and smothered my smile.

Her frown was intense.

And adorable.

"A purple one?" I teased lightly. "What's a purple one?"

She sighed, completely unamused. "A purple popsicle stick."

My smile started to escape, but I managed to bite it back. "How about three?"

That frown changed, swapping to a wide grin in the span of a single heartbeat. "Okay," she chirped, all but snatching them out of my hand, clutching them to her chest like I'd just given her the most valuable treasure on the planet.

And maybe I had, considering how quickly I'd been going through popsicle sticks in general and *purple* popsicle sticks specifically.

Who knew that the yarn wrapping station would be the top draw?

But I had to admit that it was pretty cool.

Plus, I was pretty much a celebrity with my collection of purple popsicle sticks.

Grinning, I stashed an extra couple in my pocket in case of a purple popsicle stick emergency.

"Stealing is a punishable offense, you know."

My grin widened and I rotated to face my woman. She was wearing a T-shirt emblazoned with the logo of the local after-school program whose community event they were helping at. Tonight it was an ice cream social with a plethora of booths.

Including my kickass yarn wrapping station.

"Are you going to punish me?"

"I do have a pair of handcuffs."

I knew she did. It was something I'd teased her about multiple times before. The only difference was that she'd never been arrested then.

Now she had.

And that had me faltering for a moment.

For long enough that the teasing smile on her face faded. "Oh," she murmured. "Right, I should probably stop joking about my handcuffs considering..."

I moved toward her, drawing her close, not giving a fuck that people were probably watching us.

"No, Rosie baby. You live your life for you, for what you want, and fuck everyone else."

Her expression...was stark.

And, right, I'd had enough of this shit.

We hadn't had a chance to sit down and talk about what she'd told me after the game—not with me traveling and then playing then flying home and she'd been full-on back to work.

The guys and I played game seven tomorrow night, and if we won, we'd have a few days off to rest and recover.

I'd planned on talking to her then.

No way for her to avoid me—I wouldn't be expected on a plane or a bus. I was going to be in River's Bend for a week.

I was going to find out what was going on in her head.

She was going to tell me exactly what she was feeling in her heart.

But that look on her face right then...no fucking *way* was I letting it stand.

I glanced over her head, caught Fox's eyes. His gaze went to mine then to Rosie, and he nodded, moving toward us, picking up the bucket of popsicle sticks.

"Thanks, man," I muttered, wrapping my fingers around my woman's wrist and drawing her away from the booth, away from the commotion at the school, out through the gate and across the street.

To the park across the street.

"Spill it," I said, pushing her down onto a bench.

She didn't fight me, just pulled one leg close, bending it and leaning forward to rest her chin on top of it. "Spill what, honey?"

I glanced out over the grassy expanse, remembering a time not long ago when she'd opened up to me in this very park, knowing now what I learned then—that my woman had been hurt so often, so deeply that she needed kindness.

And patience.

But fuck, I just wanted her to confide in me without having to tear it out of her.

I'd thought we'd gotten there.

Before the arrest. Before her dad had been implicated. Before her mom had pulled what she had and disappeared.

She'd come through the trauma...only to be knocked back again.

Which was why I'd been proceeding carefully, why I hadn't been pushing this...but I couldn't keep doing it.

I couldn't keep tiptoeing around and have the relationship I wanted with the woman I loved.

So...I held on to my impatience.

But I didn't let this go. Not this time.

"You don't want to be mayor."

Her fingers clenched on her shin. "I didn't mean that," she murmured. "I was just...it was a lot. Everything is fine now."

Maybe.

But I didn't think so.

"Bullshit, Rosie baby."

"I—" She bit her lip. "It's a lot to catch up on and I was hurt."

"Yes," I said, capturing her hand, peeling those fingers from her shin, stopping her from digging her nails in. "But also, *bullshit.*"

She frowned, leg dropping, straightening. "It's not bullshit."

"Would you bet your planner on that?" I asked lightly, but also not letting this go. Because I couldn't. Because I loved her too fucking much.

"I—" She shook her head, curls bouncing. "This is a ridiculous conversation."

"Maybe." I tugged her closer. "But it's also the truth, baby. It's the truth because you've been avoiding this conversation and you haven't been right and it's not just because of the arrest."

She sucked in a breath.

"Because, sweetheart, I don't think you would risk your planner keeping up these lies," I said. "And I don't think you're happy, and it's not just because of what happened with your dad and mom and the press. It's not even just because something was broken inside you when Dave slapped handcuffs on your wrists and hauled you off to jail"—she flinched—"and it's not because of the stories or getting flamed on social media. It's not even that your trust in these people, this town had been fractured—"

"Joel."

"Though I know that's part of it. Because it's not something you can just forget and move on from. But it's more than that,

Rosie baby. It's because"—I braced, went with my instincts—"you never really wanted the job."

Her eyes slid closed, breath hissing out.

Bingo.

"Your dad pushed you to run—you told me that yourself."

A nod.

"And you love parts of the job, but it wasn't your dream."

Another nod.

"And I think that part of you is terrified to admit that you don't want to do this because you don't know where to go from here. Because if you're not the mayor of River's Bend, then you don't know what you are."

She bit her lip, eyes opening. "*Joel.*"

"But I'm here, Rosie baby. I'm here and I love you and"—I tugged a curl—"*and* we're staying on this bench until we figure it out."

Nineteen

Rosie

I wanted to be pissed at him for pushing this now.

For pushing it *here*.

But, Christ, this was the same park where he'd seen me upset before we were together, where he'd pulled over his car, where he'd held me in his arms as I'd let him in.

And he'd kept me safe.

How could I keep him out now?

"I don't know what I want to do."

"That's a lie, Rosie baby."

My eyes slid closed, cutting out the sight of the grassy expanse, the late afternoon sun, the trees that were smaller now, but taking hold and growing after the fire had turned the others to ash.

I loved that our town had so many little areas like this—greenscape that broke up buildings, that gave people space to gather.

To sit and breathe in the fresh air.

To sit and talk with their friends and families and—

Men who wouldn't let them get away with avoiding their problems.

I sighed and shifted on the bench, and Joel was moving too, anticipating my actions, tucking my legs over his so I was sitting sideways across his lap.

"I'm scared to admit it," I whispered.

He waited while I battled with myself, while I battled with the words that wanted to fly off my tongue and stay locked inside me forever.

He waited while I debated.

While I almost found the courage...and then quickly repeated.

While I fought with myself more times than I cared to admit.

Ugh. Jesus Christ, Rosie. Get your shit together.

"I don't want to be mayor," I finally said. "And the truth is that I never did."

He'd gone still, same as he had when he'd pulled me into the room at the rink, as I'd told him the first part.

And held back the second.

Held back. *Again.*

"Fuck, honey," I muttered. "It's a freaking miracle that you're with me at all."

"What?" His scowl was intense. "What bullshit are you spouting now—and it's not what you just told me about being mayor," he added before I could let that hit me deep, let that hurt me. "That's fine. That we can unpack. But how the fuck—after everything we've been through—can you say that? Can you think that?"

I started to get up, but he dropped a hand on my hip, kept me close.

"*How*, my Rosie baby?" he said more firmly, drawing me nearer. "I love you. You're fucking beautiful and that's not just on the outside. It's what you have in here." He touched my heart. "You care. *Care.* Not just about the town and the people. Not just the job you've done and working your ass off to do it right. Not just with your friends and the people who've been lucky enough to be your family—and I'm talking about Bailey and Dessie, not the fuckups who happened to contribute to your DNA. And I'm talking about me and Fox and Axel and Ryan. I'm talking about how you give so much of yourself to everyone but *you*, sweetheart. You care and you do it hard. Your heart is huge and I fucking love you." He cupped my jaw. "So stop talking shit about my beautiful woman. You deserve love and *I'm* the one who's lucky to have you."

My pulse was pounding through my veins.

Those words.

They were a barrage on my heart, sinking into my flesh, burying themselves deep, making me feel so damned much.

I exhaled.

"And, Rosie baby," he said, drawing my face closer to his, our lips a hairsbreadth apart. "You deserve a job that you love, that fulfills you."

I took another breath, dropped my forehead to his. "I don't want to be mayor."

He wove his fingers into my curls. "So quit."

I blinked, pulled back, slid my legs from his lap and dropped my feet to the ground. "It's not that easy."

"Isn't it?"

Isn't it.

The bald way he said that had me freezing.

Because why did I have to keep doing it?

Why couldn't I just be done?

Why shouldn't I?

Why couldn't I move on?

The problem was that it wasn't simple.

People relied on me. I had responsibilities.

How would it even work? Who would step in and run things? Who would make sure they were done right?

Only...I didn't have to figure that out, did I?

I wasn't responsible for everything in this town, for every

person and business and decision—no matter that I'd made it my life for the last years.

I could make sure there were people in place to protect the town, could do it right and not just leave.

I didn't *have* to.

But I could.

Because...I didn't want this any longer.

That was the truth—a truth I'd been avoiding because I didn't like how it made me feel. Because for as hard as I had fought for it, for as hard as I worked, I didn't think it was *ever* something I truly wanted.

I didn't want to be the mayor of River's Bend.

I never wanted to be.

I wanted to be something else.

Something *more*.

But what the fuck was the *more?*

The bristles of his beard whispered along my jaw and Joel slid his arms around my middle, drawing me back against him.

"I don't want it," I whispered.

"I know."

"But I don't know who I am without it."

"You have time to figure it out." A kiss to my curls. "And I'll be right by your side as you do."

I inhaled.

"But it's hard," he murmured. "It's hard for all of us."

I blinked up at him. "It's hard for you too?"

He kissed my curls again. "Yeah, Rosie baby."

I frowned. "With what?"

"With hockey and my life and the travel and training and... sometimes I wonder too if it's all worth it, if I still want it." A sigh. "And sometimes I wish it was easier."

"I hate that it's hard," I muttered. "For both of us."

"Something that's completely normal, completely human, Rosie baby."

"I don't want to be human," I grumbled.

Silence.

A still, still hockey player behind me.

Then laughter in the air.

"I know, Rosie baby. You've spent your whole life being a freaking superhero." A gentle hand sliding to my hip, turning me to face him. "It's horrible having to step out of the clouds."

I made a face, but it was because he was right and because he was here and because it was his hands so gently holding me, his words coaxing me to admit the truth—

Encouraging me to move toward something that made me happy.

"You're a pain in the ass," I mock grumbled, sliding my arms around his shoulders and leaning in to hug him tight.

"But I'm *your* pain in the ass."

And then, even though I'd just had a conversation that would most definitely change the course of the conversation, I laughed.

Because I loved this man so fucking much.

TWENTY

JOEL

Bang. *Bang. Bang.*

I grinned up at Rosie, standing near the glass, wearing a Rush jersey. I loved that river blue color on her, but I loved the smile on her face more.

She was still mayor.

But then again, we'd just had our conversation the day before.

I knew she was digesting, knew she was processing.

Because she'd told me.

Because she hadn't tried to keep me out, to protect me.

Yeah, so things weren't perfect and I wanted to help her find what made her happy, but for the first time in a long time, things were going great—Willow was out of the picture because the papers had been signed and filed, my Rosie was safe and protected and moving toward what she needed, my family was here, and it wasn't because my dad needed to play lawyer.

And if we won this fucking game, we were going to the finals.

Because even with all the shit happening, hockey was going fine.

Fuck, it was going great.

Would I have liked to win this one in four? To be coasting into the finals on a week's rest?

Yeah.

But hockey was grinding, hockey was making it work, hockey was never giving up until the final whistle blew.

So, we'd rock game seven.

And then we only need to win four more.

We had this.

I skated over to the glass, leaned a hip against the sill and smiled at my woman. "You rang?" I called over the din.

"They drove all the way from the City to support you guys."

I glanced down then, focused on the kids, all of whom were wearing Rush jerseys. They turned around in unison and I saw my last name on the backs of their jerseys.

And fuck, that felt...great.

It felt amazing.

It was what had kept me in this sport for so long, what kept me going through the grind, through the travel, through the injuries and late nights and early ass mornings.

I might have never made it to the show, never made it into the NHL for more than a handful of games per season.

But damn if moments like this didn't mean something.

I bent and scooped up a puck, tossed it over the glass, repeating the process until all of the kids had them, until they were clutching those vulcanized rubber discs to their chests, huge smiles on their faces.

I glanced up at my woman, twirled my finger, and she grinned, slowly spun around.

Marshall was written across her shoulders.

And maybe I was a fucking caveman, but my cock twitched.

She rotated back around, palm coming up to the glass. I placed my own over hers, felt my heart convulse.

Cock and heart.

She owned both.

Then her gaze cut to the side, mouth turning up, eyes sparkling with mischief in a way I hadn't seen in weeks.

I turned, saw Fox and Dessie glaring at each other through the glass.

If it wasn't so cold, that shit would catch fire.

I winked, blew my woman a kiss, waved at the kids, and then I skated toward my teammate, ready to take a page out of his book.

Ready to start trouble.

Smirking, I slid to a quiet stop behind him—not that I *needed* to be quiet, considering he was so focused on the woman who was the bane of his existence on the other side of the glass.

I got the appeal.

Dessie was beautiful—funny as shit, loved sports and beer and could banter like a goddamned champ. Hell, she could make the surliest group of people laugh. I'd seen it countless times at Monroe's, the bar she was now majority owner of. And she was just as beautiful on the outside with her killer smile, her sleek black hair that shone like midnight, and tall enough to match well with Fox—who was a fucking giant.

I just preferred blondes.

Fox was chirping at her. "Hey, baby," he called. "I think that you should wipe that frown off your face. A scowl isn't going to score you a hockey player."

Her scowl deepened. Then she smiled beatifically and yelled, "I've heard that hockey players who use big sticks are compensating for their little sticks!"

Right as the crowd went quiet around her.

So the words sailed around the rink.

I barely—*barely*—managed to not start busting up.

Mostly because I had a plan.

I had *mischief.*

And that was coming in the form of a giant snowball in the palm of my glove.

The crowd burst out laughing, smiles spreading, chirps filling the air that were tossed at both Dessie *and* Fox.

Who opened his mouth. "Well, *my* stick—"

I pounced, shoving that snowball of dirty ass snow right into his giant ass mouth.

He sputtered as I leaped back then spun on his skates and...

I had one moment of, *Oh fuck.*

Then...laughter.

Gorgeous, full-throated laughter hit the ice, drifting over the boards, emanating from...

Dessie.

Who was bent over, hands on her knees, Rush jersey (with no number or last name on the back), laughing hard and loud and...beautifully.

Or, I figured that was what Fox was thinking when he went perfectly still, mouth ajar, melted bits of ice dripping down his face, full chunks of snow clinging to his beard. His gaze was locked on Dessie, and I knew I could hit him with another snowball and he wouldn't even flinch.

But that would mean death.

So...I resisted the temptation, glanced back at *my* woman in the stands.

Her brows were up, but her mouth was curved...with mischief.

And that was the most beautiful thing I've ever seen.

Fucking *ever*—

"Ah. *Fuck!*"

I jerked, shoving Fox away, who—just based on his giant ass hands—had just shoved a larger handful of disgusting ass snow into my mouth.

He grabbed a handful of my warm-up jersey. "You are so fucking dead."

Maybe I should have been pissed (though turnabout was fair play).

Maybe I should have been worried (just based on the pure murder in his eyes).

Instead, I started laughing.

After a moment, Fox did too.

And I knew it was going to be a great game.

TWENTY-ONE

ROSIE

"Hey, hotshot," I murmured, pushing off the back wall of the arena and moving toward my man.

God, I loved it when he wore a suit.

Those strong legs wrapped up in taut black fabric like the best sort of present, his broad chest stretching the white button down, the dark coat taut on his biceps, on those arms that wrapped me tight on a regular basis.

That wrapped me tight right then, pulling me against him, burying his hand in my curls, tilting my head back for a kiss that sent me...

Away from reality.

Away from River's Bend.

Away from this parking lot and the dark sky overhead and the cool breeze on my skin.

My existence was reduced to this man and his gentle hold, this man and the way he always—fucking *always*—made me feel so damned safe.

This man and the love that burned so brightly inside me.

He slowly broke the kiss, drawing back in an easy, gentle way that was so freaking Joel it made my heart convulse, made me fall even deeper in love with him.

"Drive with me," he murmured, wrapping his fingers around my wrist.

"You don't want to celebrate the win with the guys at Monroe's?" I managed to pull enough of my wits around me to ask.

"I want to be with you."

Tumble.

Head over *freaking* heels.

"Okay," I murmured, but it probably didn't matter if I agreed because I'd already allowed him to start drawing me to his car.

He opened the passenger's side door, waited for me to sit down.

And then reached over and buckled me in like he'd done dozens of times before. And just like it had dozens of times before, my heart rolled over, exposed its vulnerable underbelly to this man. It belonged to him.

And it had never felt safer.

A brush of his mouth on my jaw, but no words as he backed carefully out of the car, closed the door, then rounded the trunk, got in on his side, and hit the button to start the ignition.

A rock ballad began playing softly through the speakers, speaking about giving the best of you.

"I love this song," I murmured.

"I know." He reached across the console, tugged one of my curls. "It's why I listen to it before every game."

I inhaled so sharply, I nearly choked on my own spit. "You do?" I managed to rasp out.

A knowing smile. "Yeah, Rosie baby."

That made me feel...I didn't know. Important. Special. Yes, but those weren't big enough words to explain the emotion blooming in my belly.

"Christ," I grumbled. "Can you be any more perfect?"

A glance my way (his lips turned up) before his gaze went back out to the road, smoothly navigating the twists and turns.

So smoothly that it took me a moment to realize where he was taking me.

Our hillside.

My heart squeezed again as we pulled into one of the parking spots that lay along the end of the dark road. The valley ahead was full of shadows, trees and dipping and rolling hills whose silhouettes could barely be made out in the moonlight. Overhead, the stars shone brightly and the moon was almost full.

A pretty, pretty night.

A perfect night, I realized as Joel opened my door and I stepped out of the car, feeling the cool kiss of the air on my cheeks.

I was comfortable with my layers from watching the game inside the rink.

But I was positively warm when he wrapped me in his arms and drew me to the hood of his car, leaning back against it with me pressed to his chest.

We held each other and looked out at the dark hillside, at those silhouettes of those trees and the ebbs and flows of the valley and the river bisecting it below. We sat in the quiet of night, until it became not so quiet, until the noises of the nocturnal insects and birds came alive, until the whisper of the wind through the leaves, until the soft clicking of the warm engine faded away and was lost in the sounds of nature all around us.

It was only then that Joel spoke, his quiet words rumbling through his chest, vibrating through my eardrums. "I have something for you."

"Something more than this big, beautiful life you've given me?" I asked, nuzzling against his front, wrapping my arms more tightly around his middle.

"Yeah, baby."

"Washi tape?" I asked, thinking of the last time he'd given me pressies.

"It's a little more expensive than that."

I was frowning as he set me away from him, but before I could ask him what was happening, he was reaching into his pocket and kneeling before me and—

"Oh my God," I whispered, pressing my palms to my face, my heart pounding a mile a minute. "Oh my fucking God."

My eyes began to burn.

My knees shook.

"Joel," I said as he opened the box, showing me a ring with a huge diamond inside, as I realized why he'd been waiting, as I recognized what he'd been waiting for—

Our eyes to adjust.

So I could see that diamond ring sparkling under the stars and the moon.

So I could see the beauty on his face.

"It's shaped a little like a roll of washi, Rosie baby," he murmured, taking my hand in his. "I just happen to think this is a lot better."

It was a lot better than washi.

It was a fuck ton lot better than a roll of tape.

Which was something I never thought I would say. Like *never*.

But I was thinking and—

"It's so much better!"

I was saying it, launching myself forward, knocking Joel back onto his ass as I all but crawled into his lap. He grunted then chuckled as he attempted to keep hold of the ring and to keep us upright. "Jesus, sweetheart," he muttered.

But it was amused.

And beautiful.

His laughter, his eyes, his expression.

His love for me.

"Ask me already," I ordered.

A flash of white teeth, a strong arm tightening around my middle as he stood and brought me back to the hood of the car. He released me, stepped back, and knelt again.

"Not until I do it right, Rosie baby."

My heart pitter-pattered.

My muscles tightened, desperate to be in his arms again.

But I managed to control myself and remained where he put me.

"My beautiful, amazing, big-hearted Rosie baby, will you—"

"Yes!" I cried, losing my battle with control, leaping from the hood of the car and into his lap again, knocking us both down.

Luckily, he had those athlete reflexes.

Because he caught me a second time.

Because he controlled our fall to the ground.

"I didn't even finish asking, my Rosie."

I smiled, cupped his jaw in both of my hands. "You didn't need to, honey. I love you. I love *all* of you. And I would marry you a hundred times over."

His face...God it was fucking beautiful.

But I couldn't see the expression on it for long because then he was kissing me—kissing me until my head was spinning and my heart was pounding and my lungs felt like they would never be able to draw in enough oxygen.

It was the best feeling in the world.

But only for a moment.

Because then he slipped that ring on my finger.

And I knew that things were only going to get better.

Twenty-Two

JOEL

The laughter was loud.

The impromptu celebration of our engagement was underway.

And the boards that my Rosie had put together were being steadily decimated. There was one with vegetables and dips, another with a huge sheet pan of nachos topped with plenty of sour cream and cheese and jalapeños and beans and meat. There was also a kickass dessert board.

Although...no snickerdoodles in sight.

We didn't need the memory of her mother still out of contact, or still missing, or still on the run—which one of those it actually was still up in the fucking air.

So the desserts were a mix of things my woman liked—white chocolate and fruit and cookie butter mixed with chocolate dipped pretzels and squares of dark chocolate and little bowls positioned in between all of that which were filled with everyone's favorite candy.

How my woman knew Fox and Dessie's, Bailey and Axel's,

Ryan and Veronica's, even my parents' favorite candy preferences, I didn't know.

I just knew she did.

Just knew it was another example of her thoughtfulness and that great big heart.

The Stanley Cup playoffs were on in the background, and I didn't miss the way Axel was scowling every time his gaze went back to the screen.

None of us liked losing.

Especially considering he'd won it all not long before.

That shit stung, but it was also the nature of the beast.

Only one team won it all.

And this year, it wasn't the Gold.

But the Rush were still in it—at least at the AHL level.

I passed Axel a beer and he smirked up at me, lifting his fist for me to bump it. "Thanks, man."

The girls cackled as they munched on their snacks, as they lifted their wineglasses to their mouths and hoovered the adult grape juice down like the fucking professionals they were—

Hoovered...well, all except for Bailey.

I glanced down at Axel, finally clocked who he'd been focused on—with the exception of those scowls toward the game on the TV.

Bailey.

He loved his woman, was into her as much as I felt my existence was defined by my Rosie.

But tonight...that focus had been different.

More intense and all-encompassing and—

Fucking hell, man. My boy was growing up.

I leaned in, clapped him on the shoulder. "Congrats."

Axel glanced up at me, tried to play it cool for exactly one second. "Too fucking smart for your own good, aren't you?"

I shrugged, glanced at my woman, who winked at me.

Clearly, she'd figured it out too.

Maybe that Mayoral Magic was rubbing off on me.

"Buttercup!" Axel called.

The women stopped hoovering, stopped cackling, wine glasses held aloft—all except for Bailey's, which was still sitting full on the coffee table.

"Madame Mayor and her sidekick have both figured it out."

Bailey sighed, shot me and then Rosie, a look. "Seriously?"

"Well, honey," Dessie interjected, lips turned up. "You're being obvious."

"Exactly," Veronica said lightly, her color the best I'd ever seen it, now that she was several months into remission. Even her hair was growing out. "We talked about playing this smart so you wouldn't ruin the surprise." Her mouth curved. "There's no way you'd nurse one glass of wine. You should be through an entire bottle by now."

A gasp, Bailey's nose wrinkling. "Now, *that's* rude."

My mom grinned, but didn't comment—probably because it wasn't her cows, and it sure as shit wasn't her rodeo—just sat back, drank her wine, and watched the show.

My dad, who was on Axel's other side, gaze more focused on the TV than anything else happening around him, came out of his hockey haze enough to congratulate my friends before returning to his munching, his beer, and the game.

No surprise, considering the last month we'd all had—and him pulling double-duty by traveling down south to be with my mom and sisters and then back up here to help out (to take over) the pile of shit that had been dropped into Bailey's lap.

That was over now (knock on wood).

So...he was in recovery period.

And I was going to let him do his own thing.

I wasn't going to let my friend off the hook though, and neither were Fox and Ryan. Grinning, I snatched his beer out of his hand.

"What the—?" Axel broke off.

Fox moved, hefting Axel over his shoulder like he wasn't a six-foot-plus, two-hundred-and-something-pound hockey player.

Ryan snagged the back door, tugged it open, and we all went outside, trooping down the deck, down the stairs that led out to the expanse of grass I'd had planted for my present and future family, for my niece and nephew, and, eventually, for my kids—who'd kick a soccer ball around or play tag or blow bubbles or just fuck around and enjoy spending time together.

Only right now, it wasn't children fucking around.

Right now it was a group of men fu—

Yup. Stopping that thought right there.

Fox dumped Axel on the grass, and we all tackled him, exchanging "Fuck yeahs" interspersed with our congratulations.

And wrestling.

Like a bunch of dumb idiots, the grass soaking in through our clothes, the motion-activated lights turning on and almost blinding us.

I was lucky my neighbors weren't close.

On that thought, I glanced up from the chaos and saw that everyone else had come outside too, leaning on the deck railing, grinning out at us.

Because we were acting like a bunch of dumb idiots.

But, shit, Axel was the first of us to have a kid—to have *two* kids—and when he found out about Alex, it had been in the midst of some serious shit.

We hadn't been able to celebrate like a bunch of idiots.

We'd had to close ranks and protect him...and the celebration had come later.

"You're a bunch of idiots," my dad called.

"Well, they're *my* idiots," Bailey teased, sending everyone laughing.

Suddenly, there was another set of footsteps on the deck, pounding across the boards, Alex taking in the scene with wide eyes. "Are they fighting?" he asked solemnly, taking in the gaggle of hockey players.

"No, baby," Veronica said. "They're celebrating. Remember that secret you were keeping?"

Wide eyes that were now paired with vigorous nodding.

"Dad's friends found out."

A look at us. That stare turned back to his mom. "Are they mad?"

"Nope," she said. "Very, very happy."

A tilt of his head—and fuck, he looked so much like Axel when he did that—and then, proving that he was very much Axel's kin, he took to the strange situation like it was water skating down his back, he let out a battle cry, tore down the steps and onto the grass, launching himself into the tangle of bodies.

He and Axel started wrestling—with Fox and Ryan helping him get the upper hand—and I took the opportunity to sneak back to my Rosie, to steal a kiss.

"I don't get it," she murmured, when I'd pulled back, tucked her into my side.

"Get what?"

"How you playing at being a caveman can be so sexy."

I grinned. "We're just celebrating, Rosie baby."

"By being idiotic cavemen who are wrestling in the dark."

"You just said it was sexy," I pointed out.

She sighed, shook her head, but her lips were curved. "Somehow it is."

I chuckled, picked up her hand, kissed her finger above the ring. "Damn right, it is."

A huffed out laugh. "I love you."

"I know."

Narrowed-eyes. "Don't let Bailey hear you spouting *Star Wars* references. Who knows how she'll respond with all those pregnancy hormones raging."

"She doesn't scare me."

"Lies."

Since that was the truth, I just pressed a kiss to the tip. "I can't fucking wait to make babies with you, sweetheart."

And then, before she could answer, I scooped her up over my shoulder, carried her out onto the grass, joining the fray, laughing at her squeak of protest when the cool, wet blades hit her body.

I should have let her finish.

Should have studied her face, listened more closely.

But I didn't.

And later, we'd pay the price for that.

Twenty-Three

Billie Rose

The house was quiet.

Bellies were full, wine and beer had been consumed to abandon—minus Bailey—and the celebration had gone on long enough that eventually Alex had passed out on the couch, iPad playing YouTube videos on repeat as he slept, the rest of us moving to the back deck.

Shooting the shit and playing a couple of games.

Eventually, though, Bailey had driven herself, Axel, Veronica, and Alex home.

Joel's mom—who clearly had more self-control than the rest of us—had taken Dessie, Fox, and Ryan (though he hadn't looked happy about letting a tipsy Veronica go in the other car) home before driving her and Joel's dad back to their hotel.

Because they didn't want to "cramp our style."

They would come and stay the weekend at the house, Joel's sisters joining us, but tonight, it was just us in the empty house, alcohol sending the room slightly spinning and my libido in hyperdrive.

So, when Joel came out of the bathroom, I took one moment to appreciate my sexy-as-shit man.

Then I launched myself at him.

Naked.

He was wearing a pair of basketball shorts and I didn't miss that he wasn't wearing his typical boxer briefs beneath them—not just because the waistband wasn't peeking out above where the material was hanging very, temptingly low on his hips, but also because he—his *cock*—was lovingly cradled by that silky, slinky fabric.

"Fuck, I love your penis," I muttered, sliding my hand along the bare skin of his chest, dipping it beneath the waistband of his shorts, groaning when I wrapped my fingers around him.

He chuckled, knocked my hand away. "Yeah, no, Rosie baby. I don't have my house to myself and my woman buzzed and horny to just rush our way to an orgasm."

"Orgasm*s*," I said, trying to sneak my hand down again.

He grinned, took two strides and tossed me on the bed. "Yeah, sweetheart. Orgasm*s*," he agreed.

But he didn't immediately pounce on me, didn't immediately shove those shorts down and fuck me into oblivion.

Nope.

He left me on the bed.

"I—"

A warm hand on the center of my chest, pressing me back down. "Stay there, Rosie baby."

I didn't have a chance to disobey.

Because that hand was sliding up, those fingers encircling my wrist—

And a handcuff—fur-lined—was snapping in place.

Around my wrist, around the bed frame.

"Okay?" he murmured, reaching for my other arm, snagging my wrist, but not snapping on the other set in place until I nodded.

And, swear to God, his smile when I did, when he secured my other arm, almost had me orgasming on the spot.

His mouth hit mine, hand drifting down between us, skating over my breasts, roughened fingertips teasing my nipples, but only for a second, only long enough to drive me crazy, to send moisture flooding between my legs, to send heat blossoming through my middle.

I spread my legs, giving the man a hint.

Not one he took.

He just smiled that sexy smile again, drifted his hand back up.

Only this time his mouth joined the party, brushing gentle kisses over my abdomen, closing in on my breasts, getting close to where I was desperate for him—my nipple—but not sucking it deep like I wanted him to, not drawing on it hard enough to give me that mix of pleasure and pain I craved. He just...kissed up to it, kissed the tip of it, then kept on kissing right by it.

Up over my chest.

To my throat.

Stopping at my jaw and paying it homage.

Then to my ear, drawing the lobe between his lips, making my breath catch, goose bumps prickle on my skin. "I love you."

I inhaled, but before I could give him the words back, he was kissing me, plunging his tongue into my mouth, tangling it with mine, shutting down my brain, making my pussy go slick, my hips undulating, trying to find purchase against him.

But he just shifted, moving his body away from mine, not giving me that friction I so desperately craved.

"No, Rosie baby," he murmured. "Let me love you."

How could I resist that—and not just because my hands were restrained.

Because of him.

Because of the way he looked at me.

Because of the slow, teasing strokes of his tongue against mine, the gentle brushes of his mouth over my skin after he'd broken the kiss, the tiny stings of his teeth into my flesh.

All of them coalescing together, a gathering storm of need that threatened to level me even before his lips reached my nipple.

He sucked.

I moaned, head dropping back onto the pillow, arms flexing, wanting to reach for him, for his hair, to hold him against me. But the cuffs kept me in place.

The cuffs.

I shivered.

But not because they were a bad memory, not because they were hurting me. Not this time. I shivered because I fucking loved how my man was playing my body with them in place. I fucking loved how my man was taking a bad memory and turning it into something beautiful.

He released my nipple, took his time worshiping my other breast, winding my need higher and higher, until I felt like I might come apart with just that touch of his mouth.

Only then did he move down my body.

Only then did I get his tongue on my clit.

But just another tease, just another here-and-gone touch.

Before he was kissing his way down my leg, pausing at the back of my knee, flicking out his tongue. Then moving to my ankle, my foot, pressing a kiss to the sole.

"I thought it was Fox with the foot fetish," I murmured.

He glanced up, held my eyes, his twinkling with humor. "Maybe I've developed one with my sexy woman's feet."

I snorted, but I felt the sweat gathering at the small of my back, felt the cool brush of air between my thighs as he pulled my leg wider.

He sucked my toe into his mouth.

Without warning.

It was a little rough and slick and hot, and there and gone in a flash.

Because then he was moving up between my legs and his mouth was on me and—

Fingers slipping inside, tongue circling my clit.

And...

Gone, exploding as pleasure rocketed through me.

"Fuck," he growled. "I love making you come."

I was slowly swirling down to earth, but those words had me climbing again. "I—"

He lifted my hips to his mouth. "Let's do it again."

"I—"

But then his tongue and lips and teeth were working me again, and I was flying toward another orgasm, and—

"Fuck!" I hissed, head spinning from the pleasure, from the wine, from the love I felt for this man.

"One more," he rasped, nipping at the inside of my thigh.

"I want to come with you inside me."

He stilled, and I knew he was close to the edge.

"Fuck me, honey," I managed through heaving lungs. "Fuck me hard and deep and—"

He filled me with a single stroke.

I gasped.

He grinned.

And then he didn't show me a lick of mercy, a moment of hesitation.

He just...fucked me senseless.

My tits jiggled. My pussy protested and crooned in equal measure, clenching his cock as he thrust deep and fast and hard, convulsing with pleasure when he fucked me over the edge, milking him again and again and *again* when he lost control and followed me into blissful oblivion.

"Christ, Rosie baby," he murmured, reaching up and undoing the cuffs, drawing me against him. "I love practicing making babies with you."

I'd been ready to slide off to sleep, ready to let this man hold me as I all but passed out.

But his words had my eyes flashing open.

My body going stiff.

"What's wrong, sweetheart?" he asked, rolling me to my back, gazing down at me in concern.

"Nothing," I lied.

Just...making babies. Again.

"Bullshit," he said, cupping my jaw. "After everything, Rosie baby. After everything we've been through, don't fucking lie to me."

I wanted to run.

I *wanted* to lie.

I wanted to pretend that I hadn't just heard what I heard, hadn't just realized earlier in the evening that we'd talked about almost everything...but we hadn't talked about this.

And now my heart was Joel's.

His ring was on my finger.

And I worried that what I was going to tell him was going to destroy us.

But he was right.

I couldn't lie to him, couldn't keep him out—not now, not after all we've been through.

"Honey," I whispered, tears already stinging the backs of my eyes.

"I don't want kids."

Twenty-Four

JOEL

Of all the things I expected her to say, I would have never been able to predict that shit.

Maybe she hadn't liked the handcuffs after all.

Maybe she wanted to use them on me instead.

I preferred to do the fucking, but okay, I could get behind that.

This, though. This bullshit coming out of her mouth after we'd just shared what we had, after she had my ring on her finger, after we'd been through so much—

And *this?*

"You don't mean that," I said softly. "You love kids."

She stilled, teeth biting into her bottom lip, gaze skating away.

Which was the moment the shock radiating through my middle transformed into pure and utter terror.

Because this couldn't actually be happening.

"Rosie."

She sat up, drawing the blankets over her, clutching them against her chest, the flush that had been in her cheeks only moments before disappearing as her skin turned a sickly gray.

"*Rosie*," I said again.

But this time it was a whisper.

Because...after all we'd shared and talked through and endured, we couldn't possibly be this far apart on this.

We couldn't have missed talking about wanting kids.

But...I couldn't remember.

Christ, I couldn't remember if we'd ever had a conversation about wanting kids, about having kids, about making them together.

It was just...my Rosie had that great big heart, and the idea that she might not want kids had never—fucking *never*—crossed my mind.

"I think kids are great," she said softly, fingers clenching at the edge of the comforter, nails biting into the stitching. "I just...I don't want them myself."

"Is it because it's too soon and you want to wait longer?"

She silently shook her head.

I took a breath, held it for the count of three, then released it slowly, silently. "Have you always felt this way?"

Teeth in her bottom lip. Gaze on her lap. Shoulders stiff and high. Body so fucking still.

I wanted to grab her arms, to shake her, to draw her on top of me, force those beautiful blue eyes to remain on mine. I wanted her to tell me the fucking *truth*.

Because this couldn't possibly be right.

"Yes," she whispered after a long moment.

That one word felt like a fucking *blow*. A punch to the stomach, a knife to my kidney, two hands wrapping around my throat and squeezing tighter and tighter and tighter.

Until I couldn't breathe.

"I—" Inhaling. Exhaling. Trying to stay calm, to keep this conversation rational. "This is..." I closed my eyes, took another breath, then opened them again. "Is this about babies we would have together?"

Her brows furrowed.

"I mean," I said quietly. "Is it biological kids you don't want?" I could understand that. It would be a loss, but it would be something I could deal with. Especially because there were so many other ways to make a family.

Bailey's love for Alex, for a kid that wasn't hers in any biological way, and yet was hers in every way that mattered, was one such example.

And there were plenty of others.

My Rosie's love for her friends another.

"Do you mean we could adopt?" she asked, gaze flicking to mine.

But only for a second.

Then it was back on her hands, her lap, avoiding mine. And I fucking hated it, almost as much as I despised the huge burst of hope that filled me when she asked that.

Because it was fragile.

It was breakable.

"Yeah, Rosie baby," I said quietly. "I mean that we could make our own family, even if the kids didn't have our DNA."

We could help some kids, could make a difference, could—

"No." Her eyes came back to mine, and there wasn't a flicker of doubt in those deep blue depths, not one fucker bit of hesitation. "I don't want to adopt either."

My hand clenched into a fist.

"Your parents, sweetheart," I began. "I know that they were shit, know it would be difficult to consider bringing a kid into this world with them as examples."

Her chest rose and fell on a breath. "They aren't good examples," she agreed. "Their grief alone"—a shake of her head—"but their selfishness, coupled with my dad's demeanor, how he treated me, what he did." A beat. "What my mom might have done too after a fucking lifetime of ignoring me, meeting the most basic of physical needs but none of my emotional ones, never standing up for me or advocating for me—" She blew out a breath. "It was almost worse."

"I know, baby," I said, unable to be talking about this and *not* touch her. I scooted closer, took her hand in mine. "I can't imagine how hard it is for you to have lived through that. But just because you have shit parents doesn't mean that you don't deserve a family."

She pulled her hand from mine. "I *have* a family. Bailey and Axel and Alex. Dessie. You. Fox and Ryan and Veronica. You guys are my family."

"But is that enough?"

Because I wasn't sure it was for me.

Wasn't sure I could picture a future without kids in this house.

Her eyes flashed. "Just because I don't want to push out a couple of kids through my vagina doesn't mean that I'm less of a woman."

I frowned. "That's not what I'm saying at all, Rosie. I—"

She tossed the blankets back, moved to the bathroom, reaching behind the door and snagging her robe off the back of it. "I don't want kids." She shoved one arm in. Then the other. "Big deal. Plenty of people have meaningful, beautiful lives without fucking ankle biters complicating their lives."

"I get that, Rosie. I just—"

She snagged the tie of the robe, knotting it fiercely. "My womb isn't up for discussion, and you don't get to decide what you saddle me with—"

I stood up now, snagging my shorts from the floor, yanking them up. "That's not fair," I snapped. "Not fucking fair at all. I'm trying to have a conversation about this, trying to figure out exactly where you stand, and frankly, you saying I would try to *saddle* you with anything is insulting as hell."

"I don't want to have a conversation," she snapped, throwing her hands out. "I don't want to talk about this. I don't want kids. That's it. That's all we need to say to each other."

I moved to the dresser, tugged out a T-shirt, pulled it over my head. "That's it," I said. "No clarity. No conversations? No trying to figure a solution where we're both happy?"

She lifted her chin, crossed her arms. "No."

"Rosie baby," I began.

"*No!*" she screamed. "Just fucking *no!*"

Pain sliced through me, sending shards of glass bouncing around my insides. "Right," I muttered, grabbing a hoodie from the drawer, clenching it in my hands so I didn't go over to her, didn't continue to press this, to press *her*.

"Then"—I shook my head—"I guess there's nothing more to talk about."

I spun on my heel.

Walked to the front door.

Feet in shoes.

Hoodie on.

And I got the fuck out of there.

TWENTY-FIVE

BILLIE ROSE

He didn't come back.

And...I couldn't blame him.

Even if I had lay awake in our bed for hours, listening hard, desperate to hear the rumble of his car's engine or the sound of his key turning in the lock, his footsteps coming down the hall.

But I didn't hear any of that.

And as the sun began to rise, I gave up on hearing anything, gave up on him coming back.

So, I showered and pulled on a pair of jeans, a long-sleeved thermal, his flannel over the top of it.

Pretending I hadn't just fucked up the best thing that had ever happened to me.

Ignoring that I was hurting inside.

Ignoring that I had hurt the man I loved.

It was just...I couldn't. I couldn't bring kids into my life, my world, my family.

I *couldn't*.

So, I went back to ignoring, even though this time it was ignoring the scent of him in my nose, the way his flannel made me feel almost as warm as his arms had.

I grabbed my planner, my pencil case with pens and washi and stickers, and I got in my car.

I drove to the hillside—to *our* hillside.

But when I got out, when I started to do what I always did when I was upset—to plan my day, plan my future—I found that I couldn't bring my pen to the paper, couldn't lay out the stickers, use my washi tape.

Because Joel was my future.

And I'd just fucked it up.

Because I couldn't plan a future *without* him.

Because I didn't even know how to *start*.

The sun had barely begun to crest the hills on the far side of the valley when I gave up and shoved my planner into my tote, the pencil case following suit. A moment later, I was in the driver's seat, the ignition was on, and I was pulling out of the parking spot that overlooked the valley below, the trees dotting the decline, the trail winding through, the glimpses of the gorgeous deep blue river that gave my town its name snaking through the land below.

But it wasn't my town anymore, was it?

And Joel might not be my—

"No," I whispered, putting my car into drive, steering down the twisting road, but instead of turning left at the stop sign at the bottom of the hill, instead of turning in the direction that would take me back to Joel's and my house, I turned right.

And I drove out to the edge of town.

Drove out to Bailey's ranch, pulled to a stop, killed the engine, and saw that the lights were on inside the barn.

Bailey was up—because of course she was. Any time she came back from San Francisco and stayed at the ranch, she was up with the sun, up helping with the chores. Now she had a group of ranch hands and a manager that took care of all the cattle and horses and whatever other things needed to happen on a ranch this size (my eyes glazed over when she started talking about the merits of different types of fencing materials).

But when she was home.

She was here.

In the barn that had been rebuilt to resemble her grandfather's (my uncle's) stables. The original building had burned down in the fire, all of her grandfather's belongings lost—the old tools and workbench, the ladder Bailey and I had gotten in major trouble for carving our initials in, the saddles we'd used to learn how to ride.

Most of the animals had survived.

And so had Bailey.

So, that was what was important.

But this was one of those times when I felt the loss wrought by that fire all over again.

It wasn't the same.

It wouldn't ever be the same.

I sighed, popped the driver's side door, and got out, leaving my purse in my unlocked car, knowing that I could go away from my car for hours, not just because we were at the edge of town, but because River's Bend was that safe.

Because I'd helped make it that way.

And now I was going to put that behind me, build a life...

Alone.

Very possibly *alone.*

The barn door slid open with a *screech*, and I watched Bailey walk out in her work boots, her shacket, and jeans. Her hair was tied back in a simple ponytail, and she was bright-eyed and bushy-tailed in only the way that Bailey could be at this hour of the morning.

"Rosie?" she asked, hurrying over. "Is everything okay?"

Nothing was okay, but suddenly I didn't want to dump it all on her. I couldn't—or maybe I shouldn't, not when this was a happy moment for her and—

"Everything's fine," I lied. "I just came by..." I scrambled to finish the falsehood. "...to help you with your chores."

Which was the absolute wrong thing to say.

Because it was a surefire way for my niece to know something was wrong with me.

I never offered to willingly do farm work.

I always hung in the kitchen with Grams, baking up goodness, enjoying the quiet love, the peaceful space, the gentle encouragement.

"Wow," Bailey said, taking my hand and drawing me forward. "That wasn't even a good attempt at lying. Come on."

Less than a minute later, I was inside the barn, approaching one of the stalls.

Data—named after the *Star Trek* character, not information—chuffed and moved toward me, bumping her head against mine, wrapping my arms around her neck.

Bailey let the horsey therapy go on for a couple of minutes.

"Okay, Rosie," she said. "Now's the time to spill."

I inhaled the scent of hay and horses and *Data* then sighed and turned to face her. "Joel wants kids."

Bailey stilled, head tilted, ponytail swinging behind her, brows drawn together into a deep v.

Then she flicked her eyes from side to side. "Uh, okay. That's a good thing, honey. Considering you've always wanted your own brood of tiny terrors."

"What?" I leaned back against the stall door and shook my head. "I've never wanted kids."

Silence. Then, "That's bullshit."

"Bailey."

"Billie," she snapped, throwing her hands up. "We planned our kids' names together."

"That was grade school shit," I countered, setting my shaking hands on Data's neck, rubbing it to soothe the nerves currently rattling through me.

It didn't work.

"Oh!" Her brows shot high. "So, you talking about getting a sperm donor and having kids on your own a couple of years ago was bullshit?"

"I—"

I froze, blinked.

Because I remembered saying that.

I remembered *meaning* that.

But why not until right then, until Bailey had said it?

"But—"

"And did you forget that we went shopping for sperm"— Bailey made a face, waved a hand—"pretend that doesn't sound disgusting. Did you forget that week we looked through the book and actually picked a donor?"

I stilled, fingers tightening on Data's neck.

She huffed out a protest, and I quickly dropped my arms.

I had forgotten about that.

I *had*.

What the actual fuck?

How could I have forgotten that?

"Bailey," I whispered, eyes welling up. "What the fuck is wrong with me? I-I told him that I never wanted kids. And I believed it. I fucking believed it down to the depths of my soul."

She came over, wrapped her arm around my shoulders. "You're scared."

"He loves me," I whispered. "He all but said he'd adopt kids if I didn't want to have them."

"Oh, honey."

"But before that, he said he couldn't wait to make them with me."

Bailey inhaled.

"And I-I—" My voice broke. "I told him I had never wanted kids and I never would, and I basically told him to go fuck himself and get on board with that...or to go." My knees gave way, back sliding down the stall door, dropping onto my ass on the floor. "And he left, Bailey," I moaned, dropping my head onto my knees. "He fucking left and I don't even blame him."

"First," she said, settling next to me. "Stop and really think and remember. Take a second and truly think about kids. Do you see yourself having them?"

I stopped.

I thought.

I remembered the binder of donors now.

I remembered the names of kids I'd held dear.

I remembered my dreams of Joel's and my house full of noise and chaos, kids in every room, remembered wanting to run PTA fundraisers and Back to School coffees and Fall Carnivals. I remembered planning what I would fucking say at my first parent-teacher conference and how I would handle it if my son or daughter was struggling in math.

I'd made plans.

I'd had hopes.

And I shoved them away, locked them up, pretended they didn't exist.

Just like I had the yearning I'd shoved way the fuck down when I'd realized Bailey wasn't drinking the night before, and what it meant.

If I didn't want it, I couldn't fuck it up.

If I didn't want it, I couldn't be hurt.

"Christ," I muttered, still on my knees. "I'm so fucking messed up."

"No," she said, way too kindly considering that I *was* so fucking messed up. "You just love Joel to distraction, and now you're terrified that you'll be like your parents, and that if you bring a kid into your lives, you'll hurt them."

I stilled.

Because Joel had started to say the same.

"I am such an idiot," I whispered.

"You are a *beautiful* soul," she said, cupping my jaw, forcing my gaze to hers. "And your heart is so fucking pure. Any kid would be lucky enough to have you as a parent—whether or not you make them or welcome them into your family."

"I'm scared."

"I know." She pulled me into a tight hug. "But I also know the way to fix that."

Twenty-Six

Joel

I was still pissed when I got home hours later after driving all the fuck over River's Bend, trying to clear my head.

Trying to decide.

Something I already knew in my heart.

I wanted my Rosie more than I wanted anything else.

Even kids.

But I was still pissed.

Because she hadn't told me.

Because I hadn't thought to ask.

Because—fuck—why did we struggle so damned much with communication?

I sighed, dropped my head to the steering wheel for one long second.

Then exhaled, lifted it, and hit the button to open the garage. The metal door slowly slid open, revealing...an empty garage.

She'd left.

Again.

Hence, the still pissed.

I don't know why I bothered, but I pulled into the garage, parked and killed the engine, then walked into the house, checking the kitchen for signs of my woman and finding nothing. No scent of coffee in the air. No warm toaster on the counter. Nothing in the bedroom either, though the covers had been tossed back, and her phone was plugged into the charger. The sheets and pillows were cold to the touch though.

Long gone.

I snagged her cell, shoved it into my pocket.

Then I moved into her office, saw that her planner was gone, her bag of pencils and washi and stickers and shit as well.

A bit of that pissed faded away.

Because I knew where she'd gone, and what she'd planned to do there.

Our spot. Our hill overlooking the valley below.

To think.

I walked back out to the garage, to my car, and drove to our place...

Only, as I crested the hill, I already saw that the spots along the side of the road were all unoccupied.

Not one sign of my Rosie's car.

"Fucking hell," I muttered, navigating a three-point turn and making my way back down the hill.

Coffee and apple turnovers then. Because the kitchen had been empty and unused, and she'd need food, need caffeine.

The drive didn't take long, and then I was parking behind the coffee shop on Main Street. A quick glance through the lot didn't show any sign of Rosie's car here either, but she could have done what she usually did—park at the Civic Center, drop her things at her office, and then walk over.

So, I went inside.

And was fucking immediately disappointed.

Because there wasn't a fucking blonde curl in sight.

That pissed came back because...

Same shit. It was the *same* fucking shit.

"Joel!"

I'd been intending on walking right the fuck back out, but hearing my name had me turning back, had me spotting—

Ugh. Fucking Christ.

I knew that wasn't a fair feeling when I spotted Phoebe, the woman who'd been in charge of the audit that had led to Rosie's arrest and subsequent name-clearing.

But...this woman had been part of something that had put my woman through the shit.

Even if she was just doing her job.

Even if she'd spent time helping with Rosie's defense after things about Rosie's dad came to light.

"Phoebe," I said as she came over, leaning in to press a kiss to her cheek. "You're good?"

"I'm good," she said, holding up a to-go cup of coffee up in salute. "Especially now."

I chuckled, and, itching to march the fuck over to the Civic Center and find my woman, I couldn't summon anything more than that.

She clicked her tongue, clearly picking up on my tension. "You good?"

I nodded.

Another beat. Then she was looking me over, softly saying, "Right." A breath. "I was just hoping to see Billie before I went back home."

My brows flicked up. "You're leaving?"

A half smile. "The audit is over. We haven't found any wrongdoing in the mayor's office. We turned over the evidence on Billie's dad and a few lower-level employees but"—a shrug—"I've spreadsheeted all I can stand to spreadsheet, turned in all the request reports. So, now I need to go home and see if my business can survive a board member"—Rosie's dad—"committing fraud and money laundering." She shrugged again, added quietly, "And to see if I still have a boyfriend."

Her expression was so forlorn I knew I was being an asshole.

I squeezed her arm. "Do you want me to have Rosie call you?"

Half a smile. "That'd be nice, considering we finally mended fences."

"No more glitter glue in her hair and I think you guys might become good friends."

Now she smiled fully, before reaching into her purse and pulling out a business card. "This has my personal cell on it. Tell her I promise to holster my glitter glue, and I'll keep her in apple turnovers." She passed over a bag. "Starting with this one."

"I'll tell her," I promised.

And then I made my escape.

Walking over to the Civic Center, up the stairs to the floor that had her office.

But the door was closed.

I knocked, tried the handle.

It was locked.

The bag with the turnover crinkled in my grip, and I sighed.

Debated what the fuck to do.

I had practice in an hour, needed to eat and shower and get focused for that. And...I had no fucking clue where my woman might be. River's Bend wasn't that big, but when she wanted to disappear, she could.

Unless she'd headed home and I'd missed her.

It wouldn't be the first time that had happened.

And it wasn't like she had her phone and she could call me.

I backed away from her office, down the stairs, out through the lobby, and over to my car behind the parking lot.

That bag with the apple turnover clutched the entire way.

I set it on the passenger's seat, promised myself that I would give it to her when I got home.

But when I pulled into the driveway, the garage was still empty.

And it stayed that way until I left for practice.

Twenty-Seven

"Thanks again, honey," I told Bailey, squeezing her tightly. I'd been conned into chores.

But considering that I'd needed my niece and best friend to get my fucking head straight, I could deal with shoveling out a few stalls.

I *had* gagged as I'd scooped, though.

It was worse than the sewer main break—at least during that, I could stand a respectable distance away and delegate.

This was me up close and personal with horse and cow poop.

And let me just say that Picard (see? *Star Trek* geek at hand) made a lot of cow poop.

Or bull or steer or whatever the fuck he was supposed to be called when he didn't have balls any longer.

It had helped getting my mind cleared up.

In return, I'd helped shovel.

Which meant I'd had *plenty* of time to think, to remember, to begin to understand what Bailey had so aptly put.

I was scared.

And I'd had time to really think, to really remember what I really wanted.

A future that was beautiful and full of a big family, of chaos and joy and tears and love. And I had love. I *had* it, and unlike my parents, I could give it.

"You've got this," Bailey said softly, hugging me tight before pulling back, gripping my shoulders as she held me still and stared into my eyes. "Whatever decision you make will be the right one for you." A beat. "And Joel will support that. I know he will."

I closed my eyes, nodded. "I know he will. But…" A sigh. "You know that you're right. You know that I've always wanted to make a family of my own. And maybe I'm not ready to take that step yet," I murmured. "But I want to, and not in a decade."

Bailey cupped my face in her hands. "I know," she told me. "And you'll get there. Together with Joel. Talking about it, working through it. Figuring it out."

I wrinkled my nose. "You make it sound so easy."

Her eyes sparkled with humor. "That's my line."

"Well," I muttered. "It sucks from this side."

"That it does." She dropped her hands, stepped back. "Go figure it out, honey. Together. And if you need me to kick your ass at any time, know that I'm here to do it."

"Mean Bailey," I muttered, tugging open the passenger's side door.

"Yup," she said. "And that bitch is going to hang around until you get that juicy brain of yours straight."

"I love you."

"I love you too."

I sniffed.

She sniffed. "God!" she exclaimed, wiping both eyes. "Get out of here already before I ruin my tough-as-nails cowgirl street cred."

Thankfully, that had me laughing as we exchanged goodbyes.

Then I was backing out of her driveway.

And heading to the rink.

Because it was close to practice time, and maybe Joel and I couldn't talk it all out before he had to be on the ice, but we could talk through the worst of it. I could apologize for screaming at him, could explain what was going on in my head and that I'd been scared...

And that I wanted kids at some point.

So, I drove to the rink.

And I pulled into the lot.

And I waited.

Like I'd waited last night, trying to not panic, waiting for Joel to come—only this time, I wasn't listening for a door to open or for his footsteps echoing quietly on the floor.

I was searching for his car on the road leading up to the rink, waiting, alternating between clenching my steering wheel and trying not to hyperventilate. Eventually, though, I couldn't stand to sit in the driver's seat any longer.

I had to get out.

I had to move.

Cursing under my breath, I popped open the door and got out, the sunshine warm on my skin, my cheeks, the bridge of my nose, the breeze barely ruffling my hair as it skated over my flesh.

Tilting my head up, I stared up at the blue sky, at the clouds gathering into shapes that quickly spread out and dissipated and were lost to the ether.

I was so focused on the clouds, on those ever-morphing shapes, that I didn't see the car approach.

And I didn't *see* it approach.

I only...felt a disturbance in the force.

(Don't let Bailey know I'd gone to the dark side and was making *Star Wars* references).

My head turned first, rotating to the side, seeing a man walk across the parking lot that shouldn't be there.

He shouldn't be there.

Then my shoulders were spinning, my hips turning, my feet following suit.

My mouth dropping open.

What the fuck?

What the *actual* fuck?

How was he here?

It shouldn't be possible—

He shouldn't be able to walk free.

He shouldn't *be here*.

I stumbled back a step, nails scrambling for purchase on the metal panel of the door.

And not finding any.

And then I heard it—

"BR!" my father shouted. "What the fuck do you think you are doing?"

Twenty-Eight

JOEL

I spotted blonde curls from the road leading up to the rink.

Took a beat.

Then pulled into the parking lot, determined to be calm. Determined to have a rational conversation.

Only what I saw happening in that expanse of asphalt instantly sent any semblance of calm poofing away into nothing.

"Fuck," I muttered, screeching into a spot a couple down from where my Rosie's little SUV was parked...

I was out of my car in a fucking millisecond.

The door slammed behind me, the metal frame of my car loudly protesting my actions, but neither of the people standing mere inches apart seemed to hear me.

"How dare *I*?" my Rosie snapped at her father as I moved up behind her. "Not only did you break the fucking law, but you tried to implicate me in *your* bullshit, and worse, you wanted me to take the fall for you." She thrust a finger in his direction. "And for what? I still don't even understand what your end game was. Nobody does. Nobody can figure out why you put your future and freedom at risk. For some money?" She shook her head. "I don't think so. You had plenty of money. For power?" A shrug. "Maybe. But my guess is that it was for some other reason altogether. Some other purpose I haven't discovered yet."

A flicker of something in his expression, there and gone so fast I could barely track it. "You're out of line," he growled.

"*I'm* out of line? *Me?*" She lifted her hands like she was going to shove him, then clenched them into fists and dropped her arms to her sides.

Control.

Smart.

Even while kicking some fucking *ass*.

Pride exploded through me.

"Yes," her dad snapped. "I'm your father, and you owe me the respect—"

She bent at her waist, hands going to her knees, and burst out laughing, handling that statement like the bullshit it was.

But I was still going to fucking kill this motherfucker.

My Rosie owed him respect?

Hell fucking no.

"Anyway," she said through her laughter, straightening and wiping a finger beneath each eye. "Your reasons don't really matter. What does it that you preached my whole life about being honorable. You lectured me about never doing the wrong thing over and over and fucking *over* again. And meanwhile, you were fucking with the town, putting money in your own pocket, taking resources away from people who needed them." She threw up her hands. "And there's nothing that can possibly justify you doing that."

His face was bright fucking red, a huge scowl taking up most of his features. "You dare—"

"Yeah, I dare," she said fiercely. "Because I *didn't* fucking dare for too long."

His jaw snapped closed, teeth clicking together audibly.

"What's that?" my Rosie pushed, lifting her hand to her ear like she couldn't hear. "Because it doesn't sound like a fucking answer. It doesn't sound like an explanation for doing every single thing you said I shouldn't."

John Donovan opened his mouth.

Closed it.

"In fact," she pressed. "I suspect I won't ever hear a goddamned explanation that makes any sense at all." A beat. "Because there is no justification for what you did, and you're too fucking stubborn to ever truly be accountable for your actions."

His eyes flashed, but what response could he have to that?

There was no rationalization that made any of this okay.

She kept going, taking the words right out of my mind. "You spent your whole life drilling morals into me that you don't believe in—that is, when you and mom bothered to pretend I existed at all. Speaking of which"—she turned slightly, making a show of glancing from side to side—"where *is* Mom? Running from your shit? Or is she the one who is behind it all? The secret fucking kingpin that nobody expected? The woman who pretended to live in her own world, made a show of making an effort to care about me...then disappeared."

He narrowed his eyes. "Don't bring your mother into this."

My Rosie huffed out a laugh. "Wow, that's a surprise. Standing up for someone who isn't you? Since fucking when?"

He leaned forward, gritted out, "You don't know what she's been through."

"I know enough." A sharp shake of her head, curls bouncing. "And I know that I will never—*ever*—treat my kids the way that you treated me."

My heart skipped a beat, that sentence hitting me hard, but it was only there for a second.

Because she was still talking.

"So don't tell me what to do, don't tell me what's right or

wrong. Don't pretend that I was ever anything to you besides a means to an end."

It was then that I stopped watching.

Then I was moving toward them, moving between them, blocking her dad when he tried to reach for her. "Don't you fucking dare," I growled.

John Donovan stared up at me with hate in his eyes.

"I would suggest that you leave before we call the police," I ground out.

"Fuck you," he snapped. "I posted bail, so I am allowed to be here."

"You may be allowed to be here, but we don't have to be." I turned, slipped an arm around Rosie's waist, started to walk away.

"You're terrible for my daughter," John called. "Ever since the two of you have been together, she's lost her fucking mind."

I glanced over my shoulder and nearly laughed. Because, seriously, *that* was the best he could come up with? "You mean," I said, "you lost the ability to manipulate your daughter—who, by the way, would have done *anything* for you if you hadn't ruined that. Any *fucking* thing." I gathered Rosie against my side, glanced down at her. "Let's go," I muttered.

We took all of one step.

Then I was dragged to a halt when her dad grabbed my shoulder, yanking me roughly backward.

"I wouldn't fucking touch me right now, man," I ground out, gently releasing Rosie, still keeping her behind me as I turned to face the asshole who'd grabbed me, dislodging his hold on me.

Breathe. Calm.

Because my temper had already been on razor's edge, and now it was a hairsbreadth away from splintering.

John stepped closer, puffed up his chest like the idiotic peacock he was. "I think I do."

"Don't you touch him!" my Rosie yelled, suddenly in front of me, pushing her back into my front, forcing me to take several steps away from her father. "Don't you come here and do this shit ever again. Don't you get in his face or interrupt his routine or bother him." She lifted a hand, jabbed a finger in her father's direction. "And in case you forgot, I'm done with you too. I'm done with your bullshit standards and I never want to see you or Mom again."

"Your mother—"

"What, Dad?" she snapped, throwing her arms out to the side. "What about Mom? Are you going to give me some insight into why she disappeared? Or maybe explain why she never loved me as she should?"

"It will kill your mother to lose another child," John said, the anger seeming to fade from his voice for the first time in this conversation.

"Is that remorse I hear?" she asked dryly. "Because I didn't think that was actually possible from such a smart, capable man like you who is never wrong or makes mistakes, right?"

"BR—"

"My *name* is Rosie," she said coldly. "And this is the last time I'll ever talk to you. Get out of my sight or I'll call the police."

John lurched forward, grabbed my Rosie's arm, and ripped her from my hold.

Yeah, that wasn't fucking happening.

I took a step toward them—

"And *that's* where I step in," Fox said smoothly, stepping between us. He glanced over his shoulder, met my eyes. "I think this is where you take your woman inside and away from this bullshit."

A breath.

Fighting for control.

Then I found it again, nodded.

"Come on, Rosie baby."

She didn't fight me, thankfully, letting me draw her away from her dad, letting me bring her into the rink.

Letting me get her safe.

And I don't know why, but that was the piece that finally sent me over the edge.

Quiescent now?

After nearly getting throttled in the parking lot?

The door shut behind us, and I lost it.

"What were you thinking, confronting him like that?" I snapped. "You didn't even have your phone." I pulled it out of my pocket, held it out to her. "He could hurt you and you couldn't have even called for help or—"

"He came up to *me*," she snapped back, shoved it in her pocket. "What was I supposed to do?"

"I don't know," I said sarcastically. "Walk away?"

"That man is the reason I was fucking arrested!" she yelled, pushing against my chest. "There was no way I'm just letting him treat me like shit and then walking away."

"So, you're just going to put yourself at risk because of your ego and the fact that you wanted to get in a couple of potshots on your dad?"

Twenty-Nine

ROSIE

I stared up at Joel, mouth hanging open, head spinning so rapidly after the events of the last eight hours that I wasn't exactly sure where to start.

I was scared I'd ruined everything.

And hurt.

And I was pissed that he'd just accused me of confronting my dad because of my ego.

Because I wanted to get a few insults in.

The man was responsible for almost imploding my life, for emotionally abusing me, for just being such a negative presence in my life for so long, and I'd stood up for myself, drew a line beneath the boundary I'd struggled to erect.

So, yeah.

I wanted to celebrate putting him in his place.

And, yeah, maybe that was ego talking.

But fuck—

I'd needed to say that, needed to get it out from the inside of my brain, needed to stop trying to find an explanation or a reasoning for why my parents were how they were, for why I hadn't seen it, for why he'd been such a fucking hypocrite.

That Joel didn't understand that.

That he was pissed about it.

I...that *hurt*.

But we had bigger problems to deal with, and I needed to focus on that.

"It wasn't about getting some shots in," I said after taking a breath, holding it for the count of five. "I wanted to stand up to him. I wanted to tell him what I really thought about him. I wanted him to know I wasn't going to be a fucking victim."

He scowled. "You shouldn't be standing up to him without me."

Another blip of annoyance.

What? I needed a big, strong man to hold my hand while I stood up for myself?

I'd taken my own back more than enough times over the years.

I could deal with one fucking confrontation in a parking lot.

"You realize," I said after another of those breaths—inhale, *hold*, exhale, "that I didn't choose to have that conversation."

"You should have walked away."

Breathe.

"Would you have?" I asked silkily.

His eyes flashed.

"Exactly," I muttered, turning away. "Look, we can talk later—"

"You're not going anywhere," he ground out.

I flicked my brows up. Because...seriously?

"That's it. I've had it. I'm going."

"No, you're not," he snapped. "I don't fucking care if you think you *had* it"—a sardonic look—"we're a fucking team and you're staying and talking this shit out."

"Like you did last night?"

A muscle jumped in his cheek. "I shouldn't have left," he said.

"But neither of us were in a position to talk about this. I left to think, to calm down"—his eyes came to mine, brows lifting—"and then spent all fucking morning looking for you."

"So, it's okay for you to go off and think, but not me?"

That muscle jumped again. "That's not what I'm saying."

"I went to Bailey's, she helped me get some shit straight in my head." I took a breath, released it. "Because I'm part of the fucking team too. Because I need time to *think* too. Because I need you to know that I can handle my own shit and you can't just sweep in and rescue me all the time."

"I know that."

I dropped my hands onto my hips, asked dryly. "Are you sure?"

"Christ, Rosie," he growled. "When have I ever made it seem like I don't think you're capable?"

"I don't know," I said and yeah, the sarcasm was rampant in that statement, but—God—was this really happening? Was he really going to be this pissed and unreasonable and *insane?* "Maybe in the last five minutes?"

He rocked back on his heels. "Jesus Christ," he muttered. "You don't need to act like a fucking harpy just because I stepped on your toes trying to help you—"

I flinched, pain radiating through my middle, slicing my insides to ribbons.

He didn't say that.

He didn't know me as deeply as he did, didn't purport to love me as much as he did, hadn't woven himself so intricately into my heart and then proceeded to wield the knife himself.

I skitter back a step, running into something hard.

And human.

"Not cool, man," Fox said, taking my arm and drawing me behind him, sheltering me with his big body. "Really not fucking cool."

I didn't need a man to save me, to step in, to rescue me.

But I couldn't lie. I was glad Fox was there.

Glad he was between Joel and I.

"Back off, man," Joel gritted out.

"Not until you get your shit together and realize how big you just fucked up."

Harpy.

Harpy.

Joel was supposed to see me as something else.

"Her father—"

"I convinced that asshole he was better off heading the fuck out of here, but that's the least of your worries, dumbass. Roll back the words and revisit what you just said."

I didn't stay around to see if Joel realized what he'd said, if it processed through that stubborn skull of his just how much of a dick he'd been.

I felt...wounded.

Like there was an open wound in my belly, and my insides were spilling out onto the floor.

Like I was bleeding out.

Like if I didn't get the fuck out of there and find a way to stitch myself back together, I wouldn't survive this.

Harpy.

That was what Joel had called me for years.

That was what he'd seen me as—a bitchy, shrewish woman who didn't give a fuck about anything except getting what she wanted, what she needed, and fuck everyone around her. A woman who'd tossed barbs left and right.

At a man she wanted.

And then knew she had to let go, to pretend she didn't want, to bury the deep-seated longing for something more—

For a man who saw her as more.

I wasn't that woman with him.

Not anymore.

Only...did he see it that way?

Or, after all we'd been through, all the bonds we'd formed that held us together, was I just that harpy to him?

I couldn't stay and find out.

Not right then.

I needed to perform emergency surgery on myself so I didn't die right there and then in that fucking parking lot.

THIRTY

JOEL

"I convinced that asshole he was better off heading the fuck out of here, but that's the least of your worries, dumbass. Roll back the words and revisit what you just said."

I shoved him back, wanting to get by him, wanting to shake some fucking sense into my Rosie.

Her father could have hurt her.

Her father *wanted* to hurt her.

And she was pissed at me for stepping in?

"Dude," Fox muttered, shoving me back. "Stop and think. Roll back those fucking words."

"Fuck you," I snapped, pushing at his shoulder, trying to get by him.

But not finding much success because he was a big motherfucker, and because he was strong, and because he was thinking much more clearly than I was.

"Joel. Hey, dumbass. *Stop*." Fox grunted, spinning us, shoving me back against the thick concrete wall hard enough to knock the air from my lungs.

Something about his tone finally penetrated.

Or maybe it was the blow to my head.

"Think," he ordered. "*Think* about what you just called your woman and what it did to her face."

I paused.

Finally.

Thought.

Finally.

Rolled back my words, my snapping at Fox, and—

You don't need to act like a fucking harpy just because I stepped on your toes trying to help you—

I jerked, sending my head against that wall again.

Because...Jesus fucking Christ.

Harpy.

I'd called her a harpy and that name was—

"*Fuck,*" I hissed.

"Yeah, exactly," Fox muttered, finally releasing me, but he was still between me and the exit, still between me and my woman.

Who I'd seriously fucked up with.

Twice.

"Move."

He shook his head. "You're going to calm the fuck down, and you're going to think, and you're going to figure out whatever the hell is going on in your mind that has you reacting that way to your woman." He threw his hands up. "Fuck, man, we're talking about *Rosie*. She's the most capable person on the planet. Everyone knows that she can handle tough shit, put assholes in her place. But that was her dad, and I had the feeling it was her finally getting a lot of stuff off her chest that she needed to." I opened my mouth, but he sliced his hand through the air, effectively cutting me off as he kept talking. "And look, of course I don't know everything she's been through, but anyone who knows her knows that it's been a lot. And I'm guessing that you know everything considering that you love her, and your fucking ring is on her finger."

Not everything.

Or so I'd thought.

Because she'd said...

Outside. Kids.

Harpy.

Fucking hell.

"And anyone who knows her," Fox continued, his words sinking into my chest like a goddamn spray of bullets, an array of pain, bursts of truth hitting too fucking hard. "Anyone who knows her gets that she needs someone to support her, and she sure as shit needs someone to support her when she's confronting the man who she almost lost her job *and* fucking ended up in jail for."

"Fuck."

"Yeah," Fox said on an unamused laugh. "Exactly *that*. And running after her now without your mind clear and calm, without realizing how big you just fucked up, isn't the right thing to do."

I knew he was right.

I *hated* that he was right.

But that didn't change the truth that he *was* right.

I exhaled.

Took another breath, held it long enough that my head began to spin. Then released that one as well.

"You're right," I muttered. "And I didn't just fuck up five minutes ago. I fucked up last night."

His brows shot up. "What happened?"

"I found out something"—I shook my head—"I pushed. She got pissed." Or more likely, hurt. Or we'd somehow stepped onto some old trauma.

And considering all the shit that had gone down with her parents and her dead brother and the fact that she was fucking named after that brother she'd never met, had never been allowed to be her own person—just a fucking moldable doll for her father...until he'd been done with her and happily discarded her in an effort to preserve himself. And her mother, well, that was still up in the air.

Neglectful, but had done the right thing in the end, at best.

Criminal mastermind who'd sacrifice her daughter and husband, at worst.

"Then I got pissed," I said, clenching my hand into a fist. "I took off, calmed down, came to terms with some heavy shit, and went back to find her, and she wasn't there. I spent all morning looking for her, only to give up and come here, and—" I shook my head.

"Only to come here and find her with her dad."

I sighed, nodded. "Fuck, man."

"You need to talk to her. Calmly. Without criminals around and without a potential audience. And you need to get your fucking head out of your ass."

I hated that he was also right about this.

But because he *was* right, I didn't put my fist through his face like I wanted.

I just nodded.

"And you need to apologize." He nodded toward my pocket. "Like, you need to pull out your phone right now, and call her and apologize for being a dick. And if she doesn't pick up, then you need to leave a message. *And* fucking text her." His eyes narrowed. "And then you're going to think of all the ways you're going to make this series of fuckups right, but you're going to do it while getting dressed and in between drills because we have practice and you need to get through that first."

"Coach would—"

Fox shrugged. "Coach would let you go if you really needed to go, we both know that, man." A sigh. "But you know what your woman would think about putting aside your responsibilities and obligations in order to do something you wanted."

He didn't get that my Rosie was my biggest responsibility.

That hockey was the obligation.

The obligation that was threatening to take me away from something I wanted, from somewhere I needed to be.

That wasn't the fucking ice.

That wasn't the fucking love of my life.

I opened my mouth, started to tell him that I didn't give a fuck about hockey—not when my Rosie meant more.

Not when I'd already fucked this up once and needed to fix it. *Now.*

But when I pulled out my phone and started to unlock the screen, I saw that there was a text there.

From my Rosie.

Go to practice. We'll talk later.

Six words that I read.

But I could hear the ice in them.

Fuck.

I swiped the text out of the way, hit her contact number.

It rang once then went to voicemail.

"Fuck," I muttered, moving away from Fox, my teammate finally letting me move by him.

Probably because I'd gotten my head out of my ass and was trying to fix my shit.

I dialed again.

Got voicemail. Again.

"Rosie baby," I rasped after the beep. "I'm sorry. I—" A thousand excuses flew through my mind in an instant—I didn't mean it, it was a shitty choice of words, I was worried and upset—but none of them were good enough.

None of them justified the line I'd crossed.

Maybe from the outside, it seemed small.

I'd danced around a nickname—hadn't actually called her that.

But it was fucking *close enough.*

Because that name had represented the woman I'd thought she was.

It didn't represent the woman she'd let me see, that big beautiful heart inside.

Which meant that after all we'd been through, after the closeness we'd strived for, after the love we'd fought for...

I just told her it all meant nothing.

THIRTY-ONE

ROSIE

I couldn't go back to Bailey's, couldn't dump more shit on her.

I couldn't go back to Joel's house—to our house. *No*, to *his* house.

I couldn't go to our place, couldn't look over our hillside, and deal with this wound in my belly.

I couldn't go to the office, couldn't lose myself in work, not when I'd spent the last weeks starting to put the pieces in play so I could step back.

Yanking responsibilities out from beneath the people I'd put in place to take them on.

Such good leadership that would be.

Sighing, I dropped my head onto my steering wheel, and tried to blink back the tears, to pretend they weren't streaming down my cheeks.

Same as I was trying to pretend I wasn't bleeding out on the side of the road, having pulled over because I couldn't see, because I couldn't risk other people driving like an idiot unable to see, because I didn't want to be responsible for hurting someone just because it felt like my heart was shattering inside my chest.

God, it hurt.

But...

I'd get over it.

I always did.

I'd move on.

I always did.

I sniffed indelicately, wiped the back of my arm across the nose and cheeks—thanking the universe that I hadn't bothered with makeup, that I might be a mess, might have a hole in my heart that would never heal, but at least I wouldn't have raccoon eyes.

"Okay, Rosie," I whispered. "Think."

I pulled my phone out, jabbed out a text.

Buying me some time.

Locking down the shield, closing down the walls, burying the hurt.

Until I could breathe.

Only, when I'd just regained the ability to reuse my lungs, my cell rang, Joel's name and picture coming up on the screen.

I couldn't.

I hit the button at the side, rejected the call.

Repeated the process when he phoned back all of ten seconds later.

I couldn't talk to him yet.

I wasn't ready.

I—

The knock at my window had me jumping, nearly dropping my phone I was trying to turn off. I swiveled, saw that Dessie was standing outside my car.

The worst possible person to be there, aside from Bailey.

Because she would see *right* through any bullshit I tried to pedal.

"Open the door!" she called.

Right.

She even saw it through the window.

I sighed, hit the locks, and then she was pulling the door open, crouching in the opening. "Spill it, Rosie. Right fucking now."

The concern in her voice was a stopgap, packing that wound with gauze, halting most of the bleeding.

"Oh, Dessie," I whispered, eyes immediately welling up again. "It's all such a mess."

And then I was leaning forward, would have fallen into her arms if not for the seat belt.

And...I was sobbing.

———

"That's a mess," Dessie murmured, after she'd unbuckled my seat belt, walked me around the driver's seat, and driven me back to her place. "But you and Joel—" I looked up from my mug of tea, holding the steaming liquid like it was the lifeline it was—mostly because the shot of rum that Dessie had poured in there.

Yes, it was midday.

Yes, I was day drinking.

No, I didn't give a fuck.

I needed the burn of alcohol down my throat to erase the flames in my belly. I needed the slight fuzzy feeling in my mind to forget Joel's face when he'd accused me of being a harpy.

Dessie's hand came to mine, gently peeling my fingers free, extracting the mug from my grip and setting it on the table.

Her fingers wove around mine.

"You and Joel are good together," she murmured. "So, I know that you'll get through this. But honey..." She hesitated.

"What?"

"This stuff about kids...it's—"

"What?" I asked again when she broke off, when she clamped

her feet together, some of my misery fading because my friend was upset. "What's the matter?"

A sigh. "It's nothing. Well"—she tilted her head from side to side—"it's something, but we can talk about that later."

I didn't want to talk about it later.

I wanted to talk about it now.

Mostly because that would mean that I didn't need to talk about me.

But Dessie didn't give me that chance. She just squeezed my hand again, leaned a little closer. "I agree with Bailey about the kids and the conversations and the names we picked out together. I agree that you probably twisted that in your head to protect yourself, to have that out. I just...are you sure? Because I don't think this is something you can flip-flop on." She made a face. "In fact, I *know* it isn't."

Now I was covering her hand with my own, lacing our fingers together and squeezing lightly. "I'm sure. About kids. About Joel. I just...had a moment, and another one about what Joel said. And I know we need to talk about both of those things, but I also know we can find a way to work it out. I just...it hurts, you know?"

"Yeah, honey, I know what it's like to have a man hurt me."

My heart convulsed and all the shit swirling in my head about Joel and kids and being a fucking harpy faded away.

Because my friend was hurting.

Had been hurting for a long time.

"Fox?" I asked, watching her jerk, feeling her hands clench around mine. "Or someone else from before you moved back?"

Her face closed down, and I expected her to do what she had every time I'd gently prodded this spot before...to close *me* down. Then she sighed and shook her head, ponytail swinging, eyes going damp, transforming into deep pools of chocolate sadness.

Which shouldn't be a thing.

Because chocolate was supposed to be happy, even if it wasn't my favorite.

Because chocolate was supposed to be happy—since it was *Dessie's* favorite.

"Des," I began.

"It's both," Dessie whispered. "Fox hurt me." She glanced up at me, mouth curving in a sorrowful smile. "But the man from before hurt me more."

THIRTY-TWO

JOEL

The whistle trilled and the rage in my belly that had been burning for the entire two hours I had been on the ice grew.

I wanted to be done with this shit.

I wanted hockey to stop taking me away from the shit I needed to do.

Though, this time it was my own fucking fault.

If I'd been calm last night—

If I'd been calm this morning...this shit wouldn't be happening.

But I hadn't been.

So now I had to pay the price.

"Bring it in, boys!"

I skated to center ice with the rest of my teammates, taking a knee as I listened to our coach describe the next drill, the points we wanted to remember as we moved into the final round of the play-offs in a couple of days.

It was time to clean up the tiny details.

It was time to do our best to be smart and stay healthy—almost impossible at this point in the season, with so many games under our belts.

But we could deal with bumps and bruises and sore muscles.

We could even deal with broken bones and sprained joints and stitches holding us together.

If it meant we were playing.

Only...could I?

Did I want to?

I already knew the answer to that.

"All right, let's do it, boys, yeah?" Coach said, tucking his whiteboard under one arm and clapping his hands together.

Sending us off.

And I hadn't caught one second of the explanation of that drill.

Cool. Cool.

Just to make my last twenty-four hours better.

Biting back a curse, I moved my ass to the back of the line, shoving in next to Fox, who didn't miss a beat when I opened my mouth to ask him what we were doing.

Clearly, my teammate was more in my head than I was.

And considering what had happened just before we'd hauled our asses to the locker room to get ready for practice, that wasn't a surprise.

I hadn't even realized I'd—

"Focus, Joel." A sharp command that snapped me out of my mind. "Here's what we're doing," he muttered, running through basics before the line in front of us shortened and I found myself standing there like an idiot, not knowing what to do.

An even bigger idiot, anyway.

I managed to pull it together.

I got through the drill.

I got through the last few minutes of practice, changed, showered.

Tried to call my Rosie again.

But this time, I didn't even get a ring and then rejected and sent to voicemail. It just went straight to her telling me to leave a message and she would get back to me.

Fuck.

"Anything?" Fox asked.

"No." I shoved my phone into my sweats pocket, pulled on my backpack. "I shouldn't have let her go."

"I'm not a fucking expert by any means, man, but I still think that you going after her like you were this morning would not have ended well."

Maybe.

Maybe not.

Either way, it was too fucking late to change that now.

"I need to get home," I muttered, standing up and moving toward the door.

Fox walked with me. "Call me if you need something."

"Thanks," I said, still muttering.

That wasn't going to happen.

It was time I stopped fucking up and started handling my own shit.

How well that would go was a whole other situation.

"Later," I told him, hustling out to my car, driving by her office, the coffee shop, even Bailey's ranch—a spot I'd been dumb enough to forget about earlier, since they weren't often in town nowadays.

San Francisco had become their home base.

I'd been remiss to forget that.

I could have prevented—

"Enough."

Finding all of those spots empty of my beautiful, big-hearted woman, I drove back to our house, knowing in my gut that it was going to be empty.

But still making the walkthrough anyway.

Nothing had changed from the last time I was there.

No life. No presence. No warmth.

Not without my woman.

Cursing under my breath I made my way to our hillside...and nothing.

Not that I blamed her.

After the shit I'd pulled, I wouldn't want a reminder of me either.

But how could I make things right if I didn't know where she was, if I couldn't find her. Was she just going to disappear like her mom and then I would *never* get the chance to make things right?

No.

She wouldn't do that.

I just...needed to go back home, wait for her to come.

I just needed to stop running off half-cocked and ruining shit and—

My phone buzzed.

I yanked the steering wheel hard to the right, pulling off the road in such a hurry that the tires squealed. A jam on the brakes had me skidding to a stop, and then I was throwing the transmission into park, shifting up enough to shove my hand in my pocket, dragging out my phone, hoping it was my Rosie—

It wasn't.

The curse on my lips was quiet, but I still managed to turn the air blue.

But only for a moment.

Then I was processing the words on the preview, jabbing my passcode into the screen, pulling up the full text message.

And wanting to kiss Dessie.

I tossed my cell into the cupholder, threw my car back into drive, and then I was making my way back down the winding road, back down to River's Bend proper, barely resisting the urge to speed along to the opposite end of Main Street, only keeping it beneath the limit by pure dint and knowing that if I *did* speed, did put someone else at risk because I was an idiot and then in a fucking hurry to fix it, my Rosie would be even more upset with me.

So, crawling through the stop signs, yielding to pedestrians, driving carefully past the parks, watching out for kids and balls and pets.

Finally, I made it to the far end of Downtown.

Made it to the parking lot tucked behind Monroe's.

Where my Rosie's little SUV was sitting in a spot near the back door of the bar and restaurant where Dessie worked and lived, which she was part owner of.

My transmission back into park. The engine off.

Then I was out of my car, slamming the door, not bothering to bleep the locks.

Because I was focused on something else, focused on getting inside.

Getting to my woman.

Who was sitting in a booth, eyes on the wall, clearly lost in her own thoughts.

With a fucking half-drunk beer in front of her.

Christ.

Nothing changed, did it?

People didn't pay attention. Not really. People didn't see her. Not really.

They bought her beers and she couldn't stand the stuff.

They thought she was a criminal without the town's best interest in mind.

They didn't understand her.

But I did.

And I was going to fucking prove it.

Thirty-Three

ROSIE

The glass plunked in front of me less than a second before the beer disappeared.

I blinked at the goblet.

Then up at the man who was chugging that beer.

As he slid in next to me, pinning me between his big body and the wall.

Preventing my escape.

I knew this was coming.

Knew he'd find me eventually.

Or part of me wished he would, anyway.

Because...we needed to talk.

I inhaled, holding it for long enough that my lungs began to protest.

Then I released that breath, allowed it to escape, and reached for that glass, knowing what was inside before I even brought it up to my nose, before I even took a sip.

My favorite variety of Napa Valley.

It was tart and fruity on my tongue, making my taste buds

happy, erasing the nasty aftertaste of the beer I'd been choking down.

"God," Joel said with a shudder, setting the empty glass down. "That's vile." A beat. "And warm."

It *was* vile.

And warm.

Because I'd been sitting here, barely able to get it down.

Of course, that was probably because I was bleeding out—or had been until Dessie wrapped me up in her arms, hugged me tight, and we talked shit out.

Until she'd confided in me why she'd come back to River's Bend.

And *that* shit had cured me of my notion of things being hard and complicated and painful with Joel in about two-point-five seconds.

Because what Dessie had been through...

Shit.

It was...

Well, it was way fucking worse than a conversation gone bad and a fight in the parking lot and my man kind of sort of calling me an old nickname that was painful.

One he hadn't used in months.

Not since he knew me and loved me and—

Yeah, that shit stung.

But it wasn't—

Fingers on my jaw, tilting my head up, making me realize that I'd been rolling the stem of the glass between thumb and forefinger, lost in thought, lost in worry about my friend. "I'm sorry, Rosie baby," he murmured, leaning in so that my vision was reduced to Joel, to his deep green eyes, the stark lines having deepened at the corners, across his forehead. Worry and pain and hurt. It had aged the both of us in the last twenty-four hours.

And, all at once, I was tired of this shit.

So damned tired of the stress and the angst and the drama.

I just wanted this man and our happily ever after.

"I'm so fucking sorry," he said. "I want you to know that I didn't mean it. I wasn't thinking straight and I didn't sleep and I was so fucking messed up after our fight that—" His fingers flexed on my jaw and he dropped it from my face, clenched it into a fist that he banged on one strong thigh. "Shit, baby. I'm sorry. That all sounds like a fucking excuse and I don't mean it to be. I spent all night thinking about it, about kids, and I should have been with you." He raked that hand through his hair, mussing the locks. "I'm so fucking tired of shit taking me away from you, of hockey keeping me from you, but I'm just as bad. I walked out and ran away, and I made a big deal about you doing the same not that long ago. But I did it. And, fuck, baby. I'm worse. Because I'm always leaving. Because hockey's always taking me away. And—"

"Honey," I began.

"And none of this has anything to do with what I said at the rink, baby. I *cannot* believe that I said that to you. I promised myself I would never hurt you like that again a-and—"

His voice broke.

Those beautiful emerald irises glistened behind tears.

"I promised myself I would never hurt you again," he rasped. "And I did it last night. And I did it this morning. And I'm so fucking sorry." He leaned, cupped my cheeks in those big, warm, slightly rough palms. "I can promise you that I know how shitty it was for me to go there this morning, and I can promise that I won't say it again—"

"Honey—"

"Not *ever* again," he vowed. And it *was* a vow, one I felt deeply in my heart.

One I saw written into his expression, in those glittering emeralds, in the tear sliding down his cheek.

"Okay, honey," I whispered, reached up, capturing that tiny drop of emotion on my thumb, watching it glisten on the tip, understanding how much he was feeling this. My eyes burned, and I blinked rapidly. I'd cried plenty in Dessie's arms.

But I had the feeling that if I let go here, allowed myself to collapse into Joel's hold, if I gave him the tumult of emotions in my heart and soul that the last day had wrought, we wouldn't get to talk about all the other things we needed to straighten out, and I wouldn't have the emotional energy to address the tangle of words he'd just thrown at me.

What he was expressing about hockey...

That had been very much like the emotions in my heart regarding the mayoral job.

The weight of which I was slowly finding my way out beneath from.

Because this man had helped me get there.

"Thank you for apologizing," I told him softly. "It hurt me a lot." His eyes slid closed, another tear sliding down his cheek. I captured that one too, rubbed it between my fingers until the moisture dried. "But I'm okay, and I know both of our emotions were running high. I know we can both do better, and that—as usual—my father picked the most fucked-up moment to reenter my life."

His lids slid open, some of the pain fading into the background of his eyes.

"And I need to apologize about last night."

"Rosie baby—"

"No," I told him. "Let me say this, okay?"

A long pause.

Then he nodded.

"I'm sorry," I murmured.

He opened his mouth.

I lifted my brows.

A sigh, but he pressed his lips together, let me continue.

"You were right," I said. "I was scared. Fucking terrified of the thought of being responsible for another human. I don't know if you know," I added lightly. "But they don't come with an instruction manual, and I can't run a workshop on the best way to raise them."

Finally, he seemed to relax, the edges of his mouth turning up.

"It will be down to us to make sure they're safe and protected and raised right, and I honestly didn't think I could be that kind of person."

"Rosie—"

"Because my parents are my parents," I hurried on, pushing through, needing to get this out. "Because I was never with a person who I took seriously enough to *want* kids with." I held his eyes, cupped his jaw. "Until you."

He sucked in a breath.

"I always wanted kids."

That breath hissed out.

"Until you."

A whisper of pain across his face.

"Because I knew that we had a future, knew we could have everything, and so I shoved wanting them down. I pretended I didn't want kids, didn't want the snot and drama and sleepless nights and the stress and never thinking that you're doing a good enough job and all the other things that come along with parenthood." I blew out a breath. "Because the stakes were too high and if I *had* kids and I *was* like my parents, if I hurt *my babies* like they hurt me..." I felt a tear slide down *my* cheek. "I don't think I could live with myself. And I know I wouldn't be able to live with how you would view me when I messed up, when I wasn't perfect—"

His hands covered mine, peeled them from his face, and held them gently. "Rosie baby."

"—when I turned into *them*."

THIRTY-FOUR

JOEL

Christ.

She was killing me.

Absolutely fucking *killing* me.

"You're not your parents, Rosie baby," I said softly, drawing one hand to my chest, pressing her palm to the spot above my heart.

"I know," she murmured. "It just...took me a while to tease out that fear was making me react that way. Bailey helped. Dessie got me through the rest of it. But ultimately, honey, I know what I've always wanted, and I know what I want now." She exhaled, stared deeply into my eyes. "And that's to make babies with you."

My heart was pounding.

But I didn't want this.

Not if—

"Sweetheart," I rasped. "I just need to make one thing absolutely clear. I love you. I don't need kids to complete our life. I don't need anything but *you*."

Her eyes glimmered with tears. "I want kids, honey."

My fingers brushing along her cheek, touching that silken skin. "I don't want you to feel pressured."

"I don't." A breath. "I've always wanted them, and I can't imagine anything more beautiful than making babies with you." Her tone lightened. "I'd like to maybe get married first, would like to have some time without drama or criminal fathers or hand-cuffs." A beat. "Outside the bedroom, anyway."

Pulse settling, I tugged a curl.

"I want *us*," she murmured. "And then I want babies. Lots and lots of babies—ours together, others who are hurting and alone and need us, some combination of both. I don't care how it works out. I just want our family to be as beautiful and loving as you are. I've always wanted them, always dreamed of a future with them. I just couldn't picture actually having that beautiful future until...you."

Fuck, I was going to cry again.

Which my Rosie noticed—because she was my Rosie.

Her tone lightened, body shifting closer. "As long as you let me have naming rights because I made a rather long list of preferred names growing up." She tapped a finger to her lips. "Josiah James. Angela Ambrose. Stephanie Sabrina. Calvin Charles."

I shuddered. "That's not going to happen, sweetheart."

"You got a problem with my names?"

"Yeah," I said baldly. "They're terrible."

"Rude." But she was grinning.

And the huge feelings inside me settled as I drew her flush against me, smelling the soft scent of her shampoo, feeling those lush curves press against me.

Her grin transformed, holding a dash of wicked. "I could prob-ably *make* it happen."

Of that, I had no doubt.

I tugged another curl. "But you won't."

An affronted sigh, and then her smile went gentle. "No, honey. I won't." Her palm came back to my chest, pressed softly above my heart. "You. Me. A big wedding. A fucking *great* honeymoon. And then babies."

I covered her hand with my own. "Sounds like a deal, sweetheart."

"Good." All business now, and even more so when she leaned back enough for those bright blue eyes to pin me in place. "And now that's settled, you need to dish, honey."

I frowned.

Her hand pressed into my chest again, a little more firmly. "What the fuck is going on with you and hockey?"

My insides knotting.

But only for a second.

Because this was my Rosie, my woman.

If there was ever a person to help me solve the twisted shit that was ricocheting through my mind and heart of late, it was the woman I loved.

I opened my mouth.

And I told her *everything*.

—————

"Come for me, Rosie baby," I ordered hours later, night having closed in around us.

It was quiet and cool, the wet grass stinging my back.

But when my Rosie had taken my hand and led me into our back yard, sitting on the bottom step of the deck and looking out at the moonlit trees, I'd found quiet.

Peace.

With the woman who owned my heart.

Who would stay at my side. Through anything.

Even when I was a fucking idiot.

"Soon," she whispered, rocking on my cock, knees the only part of her I was allowing to touch the cold blades.

She arched back, hands lifting from my chest, going to her hair, sinking into the silken curls.

Fucking beautiful.

But I had to admit that I wasn't focused on her hair.

Her tits looked fucking amazing, bouncing as she fucked me, her skin turned silver beneath the stars and moon.

Taking her time.

Driving me slowly insane.

But...neither of us were in much hurry.

Or I hadn't been—until that tight cunt of hers was clasping around my cock, squeezing me, sending me way too close to the fucking edge.

Without her.

Because she was content to just rock on top of me, to tease me, to take her time.

And...I was slowly going insane, unable to flip us, to press her into the cold grass and pound into her.

Something she knew.

Because I didn't want her ass to be the cold one.

Because I didn't want her scratched up or fucked into the hard dirt.

Which was why her smile was so devious.

She knew she was making me crazy, knew that I fucking liked it, loved it, loved her, and even though it was agony to be holding still while she had her way with me—and okay, I had to be real, *holding still* with the exception of occasionally thrusting up, while holding her hips and keeping her flush against my pelvis, knowing she needed the friction but also...

Needing to fuck that tight pussy.

But even though it was torture to not take over.

I stayed where I was.

Because she wanted it this way. Because of the grass.

Because it was a fucking beautiful view watching those tits bounce as she worked herself on my dick.

Slowly.

Killing me by inches.

And I was happy to hold still as she plunged the knife into my belly.

"Baby," she murmured, hands dropping to mine where they were clutching at her hips.

"Yeah," I rasped out, my vision starting to haze, all of my focus sailing south, straight toward where our bodies were connected.

"You know if you were to fuck me doggy style, you wouldn't have to worry about my back getting co—*ah!*"

She squeaked as I moved, sitting up, losing her on my cock, but it was a small sacrifice because it only took a couple of seconds to flip her over, to press her forward so that her palms were on the grass, to use my knee to knock hers apart.

I paused.

Tried to breathe.

Tried to find control.

Not wanting to lose it and hurt her and—

Fingers on my cock, still wet from being inside her, gripping tightly, stroking me once, twice—

Pausing.

Waiting until I looked at her, until I lost myself in the depths of her eyes, turned navy blue beneath the dark sky overhead.

"Don't hold anything back, honey," she murmured.

Snap.

My control. My focus. Any hope of taking this slow.

I knocked her hand away, gripped her hips.

And then I was thrusting home.

Slick. Hot. Tight.

Mine.

"So. Fucking. Beautiful," I grunted, stroking in and out of her. "Wet. Clenching. Mine."

"Joel," she moaned, head falling back, hips meeting mine, thrust for thrust. "Baby, *harder.*"

That wasn't a problem.

I pulled out, almost to the tip, felt her rippling around me, heard the way her breath was catching, the sudden slickness surrounding my cock, and I knew she was close—

Thank fuck for that.

Because I was one, two—

"Oh God!"

She clamped around me.

Three thrusts away from exploding.

"Oh my fucking God," she said, head falling forward, cunt convulsing as she came around me, as we came together.

As we collapsed and ended up in the wet grass anyway.

But I managed to roll us at the last minute, managed to keep her on top of me, my ass in the damp blades instead of hers.

Not perfect.

But good enough.

And that, in of itself, meant that it was fucking perfect for us.

THIRTY-FIVE

ROSIE

My friend only had eyes for a certain hockey player.

She was pretending that she didn't.

Pretending that he didn't draw her focus each and every time he was on the ice, pretended she wasn't watching the way that he interacted with his teammates on the bench, how he'd passed over pucks before the game, how he'd smiled and joked during warm-ups.

Look.

I got it.

My own focus was on *my* hockey player.

But not just because I wanted him, because he fascinated me, because I loved him and was proud of all the things that he did—hockey, notwithstanding. I was closely focused on him because of what he'd shared about his profession.

How burned out he felt.

How he was struggling to find his love for the game.

How he was thinking...he might be done.

And I knew how that felt, and I wanted to support him like he had me.

It was just...strange.

Because he was killing it on the ice—*killing* it. Raking up points he'd never seen before, playing at a level and speed I had never seen before.

I wasn't a sports expert by any means.

But I knew my man was supposed to be on the leeward side of his career.

Supposed to be slowing down.

Furthermore, with the drama surrounding our lives the last few months, the stress he'd been under, he should be playing worse, not better.

Instead, he seemed to have laser focus when he was out there.

And tonight, with the Calder Cup within their grasp if they won this game, he was on *fire*.

So yeah, it was hard to focus on Joel *and* Dessie.

But I was talented at multitasking and being nosy, so I was able to track both of them.

And the longing on Dessie's face, and the pain and worry and hope and—

Yup.

She was feeling a lot, and it was all big.

I got it—more so now that she'd opened up about what had happened. I didn't know how to solve it, how to help her stitch up the grievous wound that was inside her like she'd helped me patch myself up. I just knew I had to be here for her, physically, emotionally, to be available when she needed me.

That was what friends did.

In the meantime, I was working my Mayoral Magic—or maybe I needed to rename that, considering I wasn't going to be mayor for much longer.

A special election was happening in the fall.

My vice mayor was almost ready to take over.

I'd be around to help.

But...I was moving on.

Dessie, I worried, wasn't.

Dessie, I feared, was so focused on the past that she might never find a way to move forward herself.

Only...the way she looked at Fox didn't seem—

Clang.

The puck hit off the boards right in front of us, making me jump, drawing my focus from my friend and back onto the ice, seeing Fox trailing after a player who was hauling ass toward our goalie.

And our D were...

Not in the right position.

I'd learned that during my time with my hockey-playing fiancé. Go me.

Unfortunately, the Rush weren't very *go*-like.

They were slow or had been caught flat-footed or whatever the right hockey term was for a bunch of players from the other team beating them into their own end of the ice and their goalie being the only one available to defend was called.

"Shit," Dessie muttered.

Yeah. *That.*

I reached for her hand, clenching tight. She clenched right back.

"Crap," Veronica whispered from my other side.

I reached for her hand, winding my fingers through hers.

Because also, yeah. *That.*

We held tight and focused on our players skating back, our goalie moving forward to challenge the other team. I didn't know about Dessie or Veronica, but my lungs froze, all the air within them stilling, holding my breath, digging my toes into the soles of my shoes.

The puck sailed across the ice, landing on an opposing player's stick, who corralled it from the air with seemingly little issue at all.

Like breathing.

Easy for them.

Challenging as hell for me right then.

He lifted his stick, shot, and I exhaled in a rush—no pun intended—when our goalie stopped it, when it ricocheted loudly off his pads, and shot into the corner.

"Come on," I whispered as Joel and Fox and Ryan and the others sailed into their own zone, got on their opponents, closed ranks around their goalie.

But the other team kept possession.

And my guy, his linemates, they were all chasing.

Hell, they couldn't even get close.

I didn't know if it was because they were exhausted, or because they were just...discombobulated after the sprint back, or if it was because the other team was better at that moment.

All I knew was that it was painful to watch the man I loved, the men I cared about, the team I was rooting for struggle out there—even if that struggling was less than a minute.

Back and forth.

Getting the puck. Losing it.

A shot on the goalie. That he stopped again, sending it away from the net.

Another shot that Joel blocked, echoing off his shin guards and he went down on one knee, his face screwed up in pain.

"Shit," I whispered this time. "*Shit.*"

Dessie squeezed my hand. "He's okay," she murmured. "He's okay. *Look.*"

I *was* looking.

My eyes hadn't gone anywhere but there, hadn't strayed from Joel as he tried to get his leg out from under him, tried to get up onto his skates.

But one leg wasn't working quite right.

He couldn't put all of his weight on it.

"Come on," I whispered, eyes stinging, stomach knotting. I

hadn't been in this position before, hadn't watched Joel, obviously hurt, struggle to get up, to get back into the play, to help his teammates as they fought to keep the score even.

And it was a *fight*.

A battle.

A fucking war.

"He's got it," Dessie said. "Oh, damn. Look! He's got it."

Joel was up.

Still skating awkwardly, but he was boxing out one of the guys on the other team, pushing them toward the blue line, toward the boards.

Thunk.

Another shot that had me gasping, that had me wincing and squeezing Dessie's hand even harder.

He dropped to one knee.

But only for a second.

Then he was launching himself to the side.

THUNK!

The puck hit him again and the crowd gasped, but my man— my tough, amazing, *insane* man—just reached out with his stick and chipped the rubber disc out of his own end of the ice...

Sending it right onto the blade of Fox's stick.

I gasped.

Dessie gasped.

Veronica gasped.

The entire arena gasped.

The men on the ice didn't.

Fox started hauling butt down to the other end of the rink, moving faster than I'd ever seen him move, even though he had to be exhausted, even though he'd been on the ice for far too long. Ryan was right on his heels, trailing close behind him.

But my gaze kept darting back to Joel, who was all but crawling toward his bench, clearly in pain, clearly struggling. But intent on getting back to the door, so that his teammate could get on the ice and help out.

"Come on," I whispered again.

"Come on," Dessie whispered for a whole different reason, her gaze on Fox.

"Come on," Veronica whispered for another whole different reason, her gaze on Ryan.

I looked back. Joel was almost to the open door.

Then my stare moved out across the ice again seeing that Fox was over the blue line now. Ryan was right behind him, getting in the way of the other team's defenseman, giving Fox room to maneuver, to move closer to the goal.

"*Come on!*" Dessie bellowed, the noise lost in the screams from the rest of the crowd, all of them rooting for Fox as he streaked in.

As he closed in on the goalie.

My eyes flew back to Joel, saw that he'd finally made it to the open door, that his teammates were helping him onto the bench, that a trainer was immediately by his side.

But Joel wasn't paying attention to him.

His gaze was on the ice.

On Fox.

I turned back, watched the big man dart to the side, lift his stick.

He shot.

The puck flew toward the net, and—

Thirty-Six

Everything fucking hurt.

Muscles, bones, head.

But three spots stood out above the rest.

My right ankle where I'd taken the first puck.

My right shin where I'd gotten the second.

And my chest where the last puck had hit me.

Making it hard for me to breathe, making it hard for me to think.

But that wasn't why I didn't answer the trainer when he asked me what hurt.

Everything hurt, but that didn't matter.

Because Fox was skating toward the net like the hounds of hell were on his heels—and maybe they were, considering how fiercely the other team was chasing him down.

I got it.

There was less than thirty seconds left in the third period.

A goal now pretty much sealed the game—not a guarantee,

because this was hockey, and a team was never officially out of a close matchup until the final buzzer rang.

But it was hockey. *Playoff* hockey.

And if Fox scored then *we* won.

The game.

The series.

The Cup would be ours.

The season would be over.

If Fox buried this puck.

No fucking pressure, huh?

I ignored the trainer, focused on my friend, ignoring the pain, ignoring my protesting lungs.

I watched Fox cut hard to the far side, watched him wind up—

"Holy shit," I whispered, unable to believe what I was seeing.

My friend moving faster than I'd ever seen him move, his hands almost a blur, they moved so rapidly.

The goalie was out of position, scrambling to keep up with that quick movement.

Fox wasn't.

He shot.

The puck flew through the air.

Toward the net.

I froze.

Fuck, it felt like *everyone* around me froze.

And watched that cylindrical disc of rubber fly toward the net.

Closer. Closer.

I sucked in a breath.

Watched...

As it sailed into the net.

There was a moment of complete and utter silence.

Then the red light flashed on.

The whistle blew.

And the crowd exploded.

"Holy shit," Ryan said from next to me.

"Fuck, yeah!" I cheered, jumping to my feet...for all of a second. Because the pain raged through me, my leg collapsed, and I nearly ate shit.

The trainer grabbed my arm, caught me before I crushed my face against the sill. "Come on," he said. "Let's go back to the locker room and get that ankle checked out."

I glanced at the scoreboard, saw our goal tick onto our side, saw that there were six-point-eight seconds left in the period.

Left in the series.

Left before we could take this whole damned thing.

Yeah, no.

That wasn't happening.

My foot could be hanging by a single tendon and I wouldn't be leaving this fucking game.

Fox skated to the bench, huge fucking smile on his face, bumping fists along the way, climbing in through the door, chest heaving as he stood next to me, leaning against the boards, staring out at the ice. Everyone was on their feet—my teammates, the coaching staff, the fans in the stands—and the excitement was palpable.

The anticipation was *there*.

Six-point-eight seconds until all we'd worked for was in our grasp.

Six-point-eight seconds we would remember for the rest of our lives.

The other team called their timeout and we congregated around the boards, listening to coaches as they imparted whatever small pieces of advice they could come up with at this point in the game, at this far along in the series. Mostly words of encouragement. A couple of things to focus on.

That was it.

Keeping it simple.

Letting us catch our breath, allowing us to gather strength for one final push.

And by us, I meant my teammates.

I could barely focus on anything aside from the red hazing the edges of my vision.

I wasn't going to make it back out there.

But I was going to make it to the end of this game, going to see this through.

Even if I was ready to sit the fuck down.

"Ankle?" Fox asked, eyeing me up and down, but thankfully not clamping a huge hand onto my shoulder like he was apt to in these kinds of situations.

"Yeah," I muttered, wincing as I took more weight off my foot, leaning more heavily against the boards. "And shin." A beat. "And chest."

He winced. "Shit, man."

"Nice goal," I said, trying to take my mind off the pain radiating up my leg.

"Nice pass," he said, mouth curving.

"Nice—"

"Fox," Coach called. "Ryan." A glance at me before he called out another forward's name, rightly reading that I could barely stand up, and would be a liability out there on the ice.

My teammates lined up at center ice.

The ref blew his whistle.

I stayed upright, clenched at the boards, watched Fox line up to take the face-off.

One heartbeat.

Another.

The puck dropped.

Fox won it back to our defenseman.

Six seconds left.

Who chipped it up the boards to Ryan.

Five seconds left.

He carried it over the blue line into the offensive zone, took a hit, and was rubbed out on the boards, the puck drifting to the corner.

Four seconds left.

Fox hauled ass in, scooped up the puck, brought it deeper into the zone.

Three seconds left.

Fox was checked from behind, crashed into the glass, but Ryan was right there with him, corralling the puck on his stick, keeping it on the boards, bracing for more contact.

Two seconds left.

More players joined the fray.

One second left.

Our guys were already half over the boards, waiting for time to tick down, waiting to get out there and celebrate—

The buzzer went, but it was barely audible over the roar of the crowd.

Because...

The game was over.

We'd done it.

The Cup was ours. We were the best team for this season. We'd battled through a long-ass season and injuries and too much fucking travel and...

We'd *done* it.

To his credit, our trainer didn't try to get me away from the bench once the buzzer went off, didn't try to coax me back to the medical room for treatment for my ankle.

Probably that was because he was walking toward me, arm around my Rosie's shoulder, leaning down and saying something in her ears.

I loved my woman to the fucking moon and back.

But I wasn't going to let her coax me into missing this moment.

She nodded, said something, then moved toward me, determination tightening her features. Her voice was gentle when she rose on tiptoe and spoke over the noise of the crowd. "How are you doing, honey?"

I cupped her cheek. "Feeling pretty fucking great, Rosie baby."

She smiled. "Minus the ankle?"

My lips curved in turn. "And the shin." A wink. "And the chest."

A wince, but she didn't order me to see the doctor, just moved closer and carefully wound her arm around my waist, as though she was going to hold me up.

And I had no doubt that she would.

That she *could*.

That even if she physically couldn't, she would still find a way to get it done.

Case in point?

The crutches that made their way to me just as the guys were rolling out a carpet, as the Cup was being carried out, as mid-ice handshakes were beginning to be exchanged.

"Fuck, I love you," I rasped, leaning down to kiss her.

"Go, honey," she murmured when she pulled back, touching my jaw before tugging my helmet from my head and moving back. She helped me maneuver onto that carpet, onto the ice then called, "I'll be here if you need to borrow a good leg or two."

The pain was getting worse.

But I needed to be out there.

So...I was.

Because of my woman.

Because of Fox and Ryan, who made sure I got my chance to heft the Cup without falling on my ass.

Because of my own special brand of stubbornness.

I got this moment.

And...then I got to go to the hospital.

Thirty-Seven

"I love sitting out here," I murmured, resting my head on Joel's chest, staring up at the wide blue sky.

It was one of those beautiful summer evenings—the sun still up, not a cloud in sight, cerulean starting to turn to orange at the furthest reaches of the horizon. The trees whispered to us, a warm summer breeze rustling through their leaves.

"You mean you love me," Joel teased, running his hands over my curls. "Because you get to lay on top of me."

"I do love you as my pillow." I burrowed closer, nipped at his throat, got a light swat to my butt in response. "But mostly," I pressed up on his chest, throwing one leg over his middle, glad he'd finally gotten his cast off, "I just love you."

He smiled. "I think you're just glad that you're finally done being mayor so you can plan a wedding."

I couldn't lie.

I *was* excited to plan a wedding—to plan *our* wedding.

Spreadsheets. Vendors. Cute little decor items. Customized washi tape for everyone! Flowers floating in vases. Garland and bows for the backs of chairs and dessert charcuterie boards for every table.

"I might have some ideas," I said softly.

He chuckled. "I bet you do." But then his face went serious, and he sat up, gathering me against his chest. "Two big things happened today, Rosie baby, and you seem to be handling them fine. Is that because you've locked them down, tucked away the worry and pain? Or is it because you're really okay?"

A couple of years ago, I wouldn't have been able to even have this conversation.

A couple of *months* ago, I would have just told this man whom I loved that I was fine—*of course* I was fine.

But...we'd both grown.

And with Joel, I didn't always have to be okay.

So, I paused and considered, stopped and thought, hesitated as I sifted through the feelings in my heart and mind...and *then* I answered, "I'm more okay about stepping back from the job and doing something new than I am about my dad."

His hand slid to my hip, squeezed lightly. "My dad says it's going to be a long trial."

I figured as much based on the amount of time it just took for opening arguments today. I didn't attend because the federal courthouse was an hour's drive and I'd wanted to be as fully present as possible.

But—proving how wonderful Rob was (something I already knew because he'd help make a wonderful son)—he'd gone to the first day of my father's trial.

He'd sat through the pomp and circumstance and bullshit my dad's lawyers were spinning.

And he'd warned me to brace.

Because things were going to get worse.

My mom was still on the run, or hiding, or just leaving my dad to his own pile of crap he'd worked so hard to create, but the charges had grown.

More evidence had been found.

And then my father had tried to skip out on bail.

So, he was fucked.

Bonus was that I hadn't had to worry about running into him in town—or at least, not since he'd been arrested again and held without bail. I was footloose and fancy free...

And I had a brand new paper planner for my—cough, *our* —wedding.

Grinning, I leaned forward, explaining because while my brain had hurried ahead, my words hadn't. "I'm okay, honey. I'm less worried about my dad—though, I can't lie and say that all the worry about my mom has gone away, but it's...less, I guess. The longer she's away. The longer there's no word about her."

"Yeah?"

I nodded. "Yeah. I hope she's not involved. And if she's not, I hope that she's out there, living her best life, and happy. I want her to actually be happy for a change."

His chest rose and fell on a breath. "I hope that too, Rosie baby." He tugged a curl. "Now, tell me what was making you smile. Because it sure as fuck wasn't anything to do with your parents."

No, it wasn't.

But I didn't make him work for this either. "I'm really happy with my planner, honey."

Another chuckle, but the smile that accompanied it was soft, was gentle, was everything. I'd bounced my planner plans off him —everything from which system I wanted to implement, to the stickers I'd chosen, to the washi I was special ordering, to the type of paper...

And those were just the decisions I'd made for my planner.

The wedding was going to be...glorious for me, possibly torture for him.

"I'm glad, Rosie baby."

I sighed and burrowed closer, enjoying this quiet moment,

treasuring the way he held me so carefully, so tightly. Like I was precious.

To him, I was.

"Do you still have your meeting with team management tonight?" I asked.

Joel was scheduled to check in about his injuries and rehab and to discuss his contract and future plans. "Yeah," he said softly.

"And do you know what you want to do?"

His arms tightened and he sighed. "I wish I could tell you. This last season was shit, baby. I hated being away from you, and if I play, it's only going to get worse."

"Do you think it was being away from me specifically? Or being away from me when bad shit was going down?"

I'd asked the question before.

I could see by the look on his face that his answer would be the same as it had been before.

"I don't know."

"So," I said, leaning back and resting my hands on his shoulders. "You go and talk to them. You figure out what type of contract they're going to offer, and what you're willing to commit to. Maybe it's a season," I added softly, when his brows dragged together. "Maybe it's a way to get away from your wedding-obsessed woman for a little bit. Maybe it's for as long as you can still compete. Or"—I touched his jaw—"maybe you're done, and any of those are okay."

He sighed, dropped his forehead to mine. "Have I told you how much I love you?"

"Mmm," I hummed, tapping a finger to my chin. "No, I don't think you have—*ek!*" Suddenly, I was flat on my back, the grass tickling the exposed backs of my arms, my legs. "You're meeting," I said, sticking my hand between our mouths, preventing him from kissing me.

"We have time," he murmured, slipping his palm beneath my shirt and sliding his hand up my side.

To my breast.

"We don't—"

He nudged my bra out of the way, rolled my nipple between his thumb and forefinger, sending pleasure shooting through my middle, gathering between my legs.

"Okay," I murmured. "If we're quick, we have time."

A wolfish grin.

My hand bumped out of the way, his lips descending toward mine.

And then he wasn't very quick, but he proved we did have time.

"Bye, Rosie baby," he murmured later, tugging my shirt back over my head and bending to press a kiss to my forehead. "I'll see you soon."

"Good luck."

I watched him walk out to his car, waved, then went back inside the house to wait for him to return.

To wait for him to call me and let me know how it went.

To wait for him to walk in through the door and tell me in person instead.

I waited for him for *hours*.

But...Joel never came home.

THIRTY-EIGHT

JOEL

I got out of my car, slammed the door behind me, and looked up at the rink.

And still had no fucking clue what I wanted to do.

Be done with hockey—let that part of my life go, allow the resentment to fade away.

Or go back to what I knew, what had been a huge piece of me for years. To keep grinding and practicing and working out and watching tape and traveling for hours on a bus—and sometimes on a plane—and being away from home.

My gut clenched at the thought.

But...I'd had two months without hockey.

And—

If I paused and thought and truly sifted through the shit in my head, the truth was that I had missed it—the feel of the cool air of the ice on my face; skating and stick-handling, just fucking around with the puck because it was instinct and felt good and I could do it without thinking; joking with the guys and giving shit and having inside jokes and—

I'd had those things forever.

What would I do without them?

Only...was that fear talking?

I wasn't sure—or maybe I didn't want to admit it because there were plenty of reasons to stay.

Our team had come out on top. I could secure a decent contract with a great payout. I could keep doing what I had been doing, what was comfortable and safe and—

It was easy to want to keep doing the same shit when things were going good.

But would I get back into the fucking grind and find out that all of the things I resented last season were still there?

Hence, the indecision and the waffling and—

A bird squawked and I jerked, ripping myself out of my thoughts, glancing down at my watch, and realizing I'd been standing there lost in my own head for so long I'd almost made myself late. "Fuck," I muttered, bleeping the locks and pushing off the car, knowing that my time to make a decision was up.

I had to go in, had to listen to what management wanted to say to me.

And...I had to move forward.

In one direction or the other.

"Wow, man," I muttered to myself, moving to the rink and swiping my keycard over the lock pad, "now you're trying to write fucking Shakespeare in your thoughts."

The first sign of delusional was...prose in the head?

The second was doing that in iambic pentameter?

And...hello avoidance.

Shaking my head at myself, I pulled open the door, walked inside, moving through the corridors of the arena, weaving through my hallways, passing by the locker room, the dressing room, the training suite, the entrance to the ice.

Pausing outside the closed door to the office.

Sucking in a breath.

Trying to figure out what the fuck I want.

Then I was out of time, and knocking on the door, being told to, "Come in!"

I turned the handle, walked inside—

Nearly turned and ran in the other direction.

Because Pierre Barie was sitting on the corner of our GM's desk, arms and ankles crossed, looking very much like the powerful businessman he was.

Power suit. Check.

Thunderous expression. Check.

Fuck.

This was the end of my career, wasn't it?

"Come in, son," Pierre said.

Son.

I was thirty years old.

But I felt like a child compared to this man.

Maybe it was his aura of confidence, or that I knew this man had decades more experience than me—and not just in age.

Maybe it was that Pierre fucking Barie, GM for the San Francisco Gold, wasn't the only one in the room, that Coach was there too, propping up a wall behind the Rush's GM, Wayne.

The three men in this office could single-handedly destroy my future.

Suddenly, the stakes seemed very high.

Even if I didn't want it.

Or maybe...fuck maybe I did?

"Sit down, son."

I sat.

Pierre started talking.

And then the bottom dropped out of my world.

THIRTY-NINE

ROSIE

I'd given up waiting and gone searching.

Because, God knew that Joel had gone searching for me enough times.

First stop was the rink, but the player's parking lot was empty, the public side a total crush of River's Bend residents having birthday parties or playing rec hockey or using one of the rinks for public skating.

Next was Monroe's, the hockey players' regular drinking spot.

And indeed, they were taking up their usual booth, but I waved them off when they called over to me, noting that Veronica was there, sitting at a different table with a man who wasn't Ryan...and that Ryan looked supremely unhappy.

Hmm.

I didn't like that—nor did I like that Ryan hadn't moved from the booth, that he was spending his time scowling and sitting on his ass, while nursing a pitcher of beer, and not doing anything about the feelings he clearly had for Veronica (and the fact that he obviously hated that another man was giving her attention).

But I didn't have time to work my magic right then.

I didn't have time to crack their skulls together and make them see reason—make them understand they were fucking perfect for each other.

I would have to deal with that—with them—later.

When I didn't have a fiancé to track down.

"Want a beer, Mayor—*er*, Billie?" Tom, one of the regular bartenders, called.

Dessie's head whipped up from where she was taking an order at the other, brows lifting in question.

I shook my head at her, silently telling her I was fine then called out to Tom, "I hate beer, but thanks!"

Grinning at his shocked expression, I waved at Dessie, at Veronica and her mystery man, and at the guys, shaking my head when Fox started to get up to follow me.

A shake he ignored.

Because of course he did.

Which meant that Dessie also ignored *my* shake.

Sighing, but not with frustration because these were my people, my friends, because they were just doing what they needed to do to look after a person they loved—*me*—I just slid to the side of the busy bar and waited for them to approach.

They did, like two circling lions, exchanging glares and narrow-eyed looks as they jockeyed for position in front of me.

"I'm fine," I said before they could ask. "I was looking for Joel. He had that meeting today"—a glance at Fox, who nodded, because he'd had his own meeting not long ago and would be suiting up with the Gold next season—"but he didn't know what he wanted to do."

A nod from Dessie.

Because I'd talked to her about Joel's indecision.

Then one from Fox because he'd been Joel's additional sounding board, but his expression didn't clear like Dessie's had. "That was hours ago."

That I knew.

But I didn't let the trickle of worry weave itself through my belly. "He had a lot to process," I said softly. "And I've got a few more places to check and see where he'd do that. After that, I'll call in the reinforcements. I promise," I added when Fox's expression clouded.

The big man ran a hand through his beard, the hairs scratching against his palm, then sighed. "But I'm storming the castle—regardless of your guys' state of nakedness—if you don't text me to let me know you both are okay."

That had me laughing, but then again, this man so often did that.

"Talk to you both later."

And then I left Monroe's, got in my car, and drove to the place I should have headed first.

To our hillside.

I saw his car even before I crested the top of the hill, parked there on the side of the road, his body silhouetted in the waning sunshine.

When I walked over, shoes crunching on the dirt, he glanced over as though I'd surprised him, as though he'd been so deep in thought he hadn't heard the engine of my SUV, my car door slam shut. "Rosie baby—" His eyes focused, and he jerked his head hard once. "Fuck, it's *late*." He rushed over to me, cupped my jaw. "I'm so sorry, sweetheart. I didn't mean—"

"Hush," I said, covering his palm with my own, moving into the circle of his arms. "I was worried, but here you are."

His eyes slid closed. "Here I am."

Fuck.

Was it that bad?

Had they not offered him a contract?

Because I knew without a doubt that deep down, he wasn't done with hockey, that this last season had brought some feelings that the end might be coming soon, but that we'd dealt with too much shit, too much drama, had too many things poisoning his season for him to make the decision outright to quit.

So, I knew the want was still there, even though it had been complicated and twisted, and I wanted to tell him that, but it was his decision to make.

But...had the Rush not wanted him back?

That was something I hadn't even considered.

Because of how he'd played these last few seasons, how good he was, how much of a backbone he was for the team.

And now they'd—

Fuck.

"Talk to me," I said, banking the emotion and taking a page out of my old pragmatic mayor playbook, "and start at the beginning."

"They want me with the Gold."

I blinked. Once. Twice. Pulse starting to pick up its pace. "As in, the *San Francisco* Gold," I whispered.

He winced and pulled back, pacing away and shoving his hand through his hair. "I know," he said. "I *fucking* know. San Francisco isn't far, but it's fucking San Francisco, and it's far enough. And River's Bend is in your blood. How could I possibly ask you to leave it?" He spun back around, shoving his hand through his hair again. "And the season is longer and the travel is more and they want a fucking three-year commitment—"

He folded into a crouch, as though his knees stopped working and simply couldn't hold up the weight of his big body, hands going to the side of his head, clutching at his hair.

"I can't leave you," he rasped. "Not again. But if I do this—"

Mayor hat—*ex*-mayor hat—or not, I was slow processing all of this.

Until the wave of words, of his emotions surrounding me, penetrating my mind, suddenly sinking in.

Joel—the man I loved, the man who'd told me more than once

that he would never be good enough to play in the NHL had been offered a contract.

A *three-year* contract.

My eyes immediately welled up and began leaking, tears dripping down my cheeks.

I must have made a noise because he whipped around, lurched to his feet, coming toward me. "No, Rosie baby, don't cry," he said, wiping at my cheeks. "I won't do it. I won't leave again. I won't—"

My heart squeezed hard.

Fuck. This. Man.

I loved him so damned much.

And now he was pissing me off.

He was going to squander this chance, to let his dream go, just because he was worried about being out of town for hockey.

"Fuck that," I said.

"I won't do it," he repeated, clearly not hearing me, still dabbing at my tears. "I won't fucking *do it.*"

"Fuck that," I said, and then more firmly, loud enough to cut through the spiraling, the bullshit that was spinning through his mind, "*Fuck that!*"

He blinked.

"Do you want to play hockey with the Gold?"

Another blink. Then, "I don't want—"

"Joel," I snapped, saying what I should have said over the last weeks, when I'd been trying to give him space to make a decision on his own, not wanting to take over. Well, guess what? That ship had sailed. Ex-mayor Rosie was here and she wasn't going to take any shit. "Stop thinking about *me.*" I dropped my hand onto his chest. "What do you want in here?"

"You," he said without hesitation.

Which made my heart squeeze again.

God, I loved this man.

"And do you want to keep playing hockey?"

He froze, muscles going tight, body so frozen he could have been playing a statue.

"Not me, honey. Not River's Bend. Not any of the other external factors." I pressed my palm more firmly against his chest, feeling his heart pounding below. "In here. Do you want it?"

His eyes slid closed.

His head dropped forward, chin settling against his chest. "Yes."

It was barely a whisper.

But it was there. I wound my arms around his shoulders, drew him closer.

"Then, I guess we're moving to San Francisco."

———

We *did* go to San Francisco.

But it was after that night.

And it was after we'd been so busy celebrating back at home that Fox had given up on texting and calling our phones, and had barged into our house heedless of our states of nakedness.

We'd scarred him for life.

He'd claimed he would never look at handcuffs the same way.

It was after all of that—and plenty more—that we went to San Francisco.

Epilogue

"I need you to string these lights," my Rosie said, dumping several strands of fairy lights into my arms.

"Rude," I teased, leaning down to brush my lips over hers. "Putting your Stanley Cup winning husband to work."

"Pish." She waved a hand. "That was years ago now."

It *was* years ago.

Two, in fact.

Right before my contract had ended with the Gold.

Three seasons playing at a level I'd never anticipated getting to.

Magic.

Heaven.

Mine.

I'd been offered another contract—this one only for a year—and the money had been tempting because who knew when I'd get another paycheck that big.

But I'd tasted that magic, experienced that beauty.

Hefting the Cup—the *Stanley* Cup—and doing it without a

broken ankle, without a busted rib, without a severely bruised shin (as pathetic as it sounded) had been fucking amazing.

But I didn't need to go for it again.

I could grab on to something else.

And this time, I wanted it to be with my Rosie. Our future. Our happy ending. Our big, beautiful life together without being tied to a city, to a training schedule, to my responsibilities as a teammate.

It was glorious.

We'd traveled.

We'd fucked on a private beach in the south of France. We'd fucked in a castle in Scotland. We'd fucked freezing our asses off while the Northern Lights glowed overhead.

Cruises and plane rides.

Road trips and national parks.

And time.

Just the two of us.

Now we were back in River's Bend—well, not right now because we were actually in a small vineyard an hour's drive south of town.

And I was stringing twinkly lights.

"Are you going to come behind me and micromanage me as I hang them?"

She grinned, rose up on tiptoe, and pressed her mouth to mine. "Of course I am."

Because my woman was all about the details.

And because she was killing it as the premier wedding planner in the region—planning everything from small, intimate ceremonies for our friends (like this one), to huge four hundred guest ceremonies that took place over long weekends and were planned from top to tail with expensive events.

(Part of the reason I hadn't needed that big-ass NHL paycheck).

She had her spreadsheets.

And planners and washi and stickers.

She also just had silk ribbons and fairy lights and six-layer cakes.

And even more spreadsheets.

"I'd better get to work then," I teased.

"Damn right, you do." She patted me on the ass. "Get that cute butt to work." She started to turn away—

I caught her around the waist, drew her back to me, smoothing my hand over her belly.

Over the *rounded* curve of her belly.

Because she might be killing it as the premier wedding planner in the region and I might be a retired Stanley Cup winning hockey player, but we'd also had our time together.

And now...we were building a future.

With twins.

My Rosie was thirty-two weeks pregnant, in full-on waddle mode, but nothing had ever stopped her, and neither did carrying two babies.

This was her last wedding for six months—and she'd only done it because our friends, our family, had needed help. They hadn't asked, knowing exactly how far fuck along she would be when it came to the day that they exchanged their vows.

But they're my Rosie's family.

My family.

And this was the way she showed her love.

So she'd stepped in, wouldn't take no for an answer, and now their day would be beautiful.

Because of family and love and my Rosie.

And with the rest of us put to work picking up personalized cookies and making flower arrangements and stringing fairy lights and tying and retying the bows on the chair covers—*all* of us were working.

But I had the biggest job, minus the lights:

Following my woman around and making sure she didn't overdo it (as much as that would ever be possible with my Rosie).

I loved that job.

Loved *her*.

Plus, I still loved her ass, clad in that tight blue dress.

"Back to work," she called, catching me looking. "Or no handcuffs later."

A groan came from somewhere behind me. "God, no, not the handcuffs."

I grinned.

But Rosie, my Rosie, was always on her toes, always ready. "Those handcuffs made these babies"—another groan that had her winking at me—"and now"—a narrow-eyed stare before she clapped her hands—"back to work!"

Mayoral Magic.

Wedding Planner Witchcraft.

Just...

My Rosie.

My perfect, beautiful Rosie.

Who owned my heart.

Who owned my soul.

Who turned that narrow-eyed stare on me...and got me back to stringing those fairy lights.

———

Fox, Five Years Before

I wanted to rinse my eyes out with acid.

Then I wanted to gouge them out with a spoon.

I'd been worried about Joel, about the look in Rosie's eyes when she'd walked into Monroe's, looking for him after his meeting with Rush management

And she hadn't texted.

Neither had he.

Or replied to mine.

Or picked up any of my calls.

And trouble followed those two like it was a fucking note taped to each of their backs.

So...I'd gone to their house, just intending to take a peek inside, to make sure Rosie and Joel had connected and they were both okay.

And—

I shuddered.

Well, I sure as shit had gotten my peek.

And more.

I gagged, shook myself, and kept making my way along the tree line.

Kept making my way *through* the trees, to the spot I needed to check.

Because there was another reason I was on this side of town, another reason I was well away from my apartment in downtown River's Bend.

An apartment I'd just broken my lease on.

Because I was going to San Francisco.

Finally, I was getting a contract.

Finally, I was going to consistently play at the highest level of hockey possible.

But not tonight.

Tonight I was dealing with acid-filled eyes and spoons made for gouging and a sick feeling in the pit of my stomach that had nothing to do with walking in on my friends fucking.

With handcuffs.

Another shudder.

"Focus," I muttered, even though I didn't want to, even though I'd been avoiding thinking about this shit for far too fucking long—not wanting to admit what was right in front of me...

Even though it was *right in front of me.*

And then I'd confirmed it.

But then I couldn't do anything about it—not with all the shit swirling through River's Bend, not with my own life equally a mess.

Not with...

Dessie being Dessie.

I cursed under my breath, knowing this was all a nightmare that was going to blow up on me, doing more damage than acid and dulled spoons.

But still walking to the spot the note slipped under the windshield wiper of my car outside Monroe's had said.

"Probably going to get murdered out here," I muttered. "Probably some sick joke."

Only...I knew it wasn't.

Because when I rounded the corner of the trail, eyes having long adjusted to the dark, I could easily see the person silhouetted against the moonlight in the small clearing.

A clearing I vaguely remembered.

From decades before.

The person on the other side of it turned, and I felt that same gut punch as I'd experienced the first time I saw her.

Only this one was more powerful.

I knew for certain now.

Which was why I moved close enough to see her face, her expression, her eyes that were a familiar shade of blue I'd seen so often during my time with the Rush.

Which was why I moved close to Annie Donovan.

Moved close to Rosie's mother.

And because the name I'd been born with wasn't actually Fox, I said, "Hi, Mom."

She opened her mouth to reply—

A gasp.

From *behind me.*

I turned...
Dessie was standing directly behind me.

————

Thank you for reading! I hope you enjoyed Rosie and Joel's story as much as I loved writing their rollercoaster of a journey! Fox and Dessie's story begins in PUCK AND MAKE UP. **I'm not the type to settle down...except for her.**
CLICK HERE TO READ PUCK AND MAKE UP NOW>

————

And don't miss book one in my brand new hockey series, OVER THE LINE. **I'm snowed in. With a famous hockey player.**
My life has been a disaster. I've lost my job, my apartment, and my direction, so when my best friend suggests a week trip up to her house in Tahoe, I jump on the chance for a change in scenery.
Only, I didn't anticipate Snowmageddon.
I didn't anticipate being trapped on the side of the road and rescued by a famous hockey player—and certainly not by Lake Jordan, star center for the Sierra Hockey team, model, and entrepreneur.
I didn't anticipate having to share his house.
Or that there would only be one bedroom.
And I didn't anticipate...that he might want to keep me.
Forever.
CLICK HERE TO READ OVER THE LINE NOW>

————

And if you enjoyed NO PUCKS LOST BETWEEN US, you'll love BROKEN LACES, book 1 of my new series, the Eagles

Hockey series. **This team of misfits and bad boys are going to puck you in the best possible way.**

CLICK HERE TO READ BROKEN LACES NOW>

———

I so appreciate your help in spreading the word about my books, including sharing with friends! Please leave a review on your favorite book site!

You can also join my Facebook group, the Fabinators, for exclusive giveaways and sneak peeks of future books.

If you'd like to receive emails from me for new releases and monthly giveaway sign up for my newsletter at https://www.elise faber.com/newsletter

Hate missing Elise's new releases? Love contests, exclusive excerpts and giveaways?
Then signup for Elise's newsletter here!

www.elisefaber.com/newsletter

––––––

And join Elise's fan group, the Fabinators (https://www.facebook.com/groups/fabinators) for insider information, sneak peaks at new releases, and fun freebies! Hope to see you there!

––––––

If you enjoy my series, considering supporting me on PATREON! Get access to early releases, bonus content, character art, audiobooks, special edition covers, swag, and much more!

CLICK HERE TO SUPPORT ME>

––––––

I so appreciate your help in spreading the word about my books, including sharing with friends! Please leave a review on your favorite book site!

Rush Hockey

Big Puck Energy
Filthy Puckboy
So Pucking Over It
Love, Pucks, and Other Stories
All's Fair in Pucks and War
No Pucks Lost Between Us
Puck and Make Up
Blinded By Pucks
Match Made in Pucks

Blocked

Backhand

Boarding

Benched

Breakaway

Breakout

Checked

Coasting

Centered

Charging

Caged

Crashed

A Gold Christmas

Cycled

Caught

Cap

Covered

Crushed

Changed

Scored

Breakers Hockey (all stand alone)

Broken

Boldly

Breathless

Ballsy

Bewitched

Blowout

Breathe

Blazed

Sierra Hockey Series

Over the Line

The Big Skate

Caught from Behind

On the Fly

Rush Hockey Trilogy #1

Big Puck Energy

Filthy Puckboy

So Pucking Over It

Rush Hockey Trilogy #2

Love, Pucks, and Other Stories

All's Fair in Pucks and War

No Pucks Lost Between Us

Rush Hockey Trilogy #3

Puck and Make Up

Blinded By Pucks

Match Made in Pucks

Eagles Hockey Series (all stand alone)

Broken Laces

Knotted Laces

Lace 'em Up

Love, Action, Camera (all stand alone)

Dotted Line

Action Shot

Close-Up

End Scene

Meet Cute

Love After Midnight **(all stand alone)**

Rum And Notes

Virgin Daiquiri

On The Rocks

Sex On The Seats

Life Sucks Series

Train Wreck

Hot Mess

Dumpster Fire

Clusterf*@k

FUBAR

Perfect Storm

Free Fall

Lost Cause

Roosevelt Ranch Series **(all stand alone, series complete)**

Disaster at Roosevelt Ranch

Heartbreak at Roosevelt Ranch

Collision at Roosevelt Ranch

Regret at Roosevelt Ranch

Desire at Roosevelt Ranch

***Phoenix Series* (read in order)**

Phoenix Rising

Dark Phoenix

Phoenix Freed

***Phoenix: LexTal Chronicles* (rereleasing soon, stand alone, Phoenix world)**

From Ashes

In Flames

To Smoke

KTS Series (all stand alone, series complete)

Riding The Edge

Crossing The Line

Leveling The Field

Scorching The Earth

Cocky Heroes World

Tattooed Troublemaker

ABOUT THE AUTHOR

USA Today bestselling author, Elise Faber, loves chocolate, Star Wars, Harry Potter, and hockey (the order depending on the day and how well her team -- the Sharks! -- are playing). She and her husband also play as much hockey as they can squeeze into their schedules, so much so that their typical date night is spent on the ice. Elise is the mom to two exuberant boys and lives in Northern California. Connect with her in her Facebook group, the Fabinators or find more information about her books at www.elise-faber.com.

facebook.com/elisefaberauthor

amazon.com/author/elisefaber

bookbub.com/profile/elise-faber

instagram.com/elisefaber

tiktok.com/@elisefaberauthor

goodreads.com/elisefaber